C000044717

# DON'T TELL A SOUL

# ALSO BY NICK SANDS

*Le... ...ty Footprints*

# DON'T
# TELL
# A SOUL

Nick Sands

Copyright © 2023 Nick Sands

The moral right of the author has been asserted.

Apart from any fair dealing for the purposes of research or private study,
or criticism or review, as permitted under the Copyright, Designs and Patents
Act 1988, this publication may only be reproduced, stored or transmitted, in
any form or by any means, with the prior permission in writing of the
publishers, or in the case of reprographic reproduction in accordance with
the terms of licences issued by the Copyright Licensing Agency. Enquiries
concerning reproduction outside those terms should be sent to the publishers.

This is a work of fiction. Names, characters, businesses, places, events
and incidents are either the products of the author's imagination
or used in a fictitious manner. Any resemblance to actual persons,
living or dead, or actual events is purely coincidental.

Matador
Unit E2 Airfield Business Park,
Harrison Road, Market Harborough,
Leicestershire. LE16 7UL
Tel: 0116 2792299
Email: books@troubador.co.uk
Web: www.troubador.co.uk/matador
Twitter: @matadorbooks

ISBN 978 1805141 518

British Library Cataloguing in Publication Data.
A catalogue record for this book is available from the British Library.

Printed and bound in Great Britain by 4edge Limited
Typeset in 11pt Minion Pro by Troubador Publishing Ltd, Leicester, UK

Matador is an imprint of Troubador Publishing Ltd

For Claire and Chris

# THE CAST

MATT CRAWFORD – private detective
KATE BROOKS – Matt's assistant
DESMOND – Matt's cat
AMANDA COLES – Matt's ex-wife
LUKE BROOKS – Kate's husband
JASMINE – Kate's friend
STEVE MACKIE – estate agent
HAZEL MACKIE – Steve's wife
FIONA CAMPBELL – Hazel's friend
MONICA PURVIS – Steve's secretary
BRIAN HENSON – Steve's client
GUY TRAVERS – Steve's accountant
KEN MARCHANT – property developer
HARRY BARTON – Steve's friend
LINDA BARTON – Harry's wife
EDDIE FLETCHER – rowing club manager

ELLIE PRICE – mother of Steve's late friend Carl Price

FATHER ANTHONY MOSS – Catholic priest

DI JOE MARTIN – leading the police investigation

DS ANDY CROWTHER – DI Martin's sidekick

DCI RICHARD CRAWFORD – Matt's older brother (Vice Squad)

DS DIANE COLLINS – Carl Price's ex-fiancée

KEITH FERRELL – local press reporter

JACK GREAVES – police informer

MICHAEL SHANAHAN – owner of the Dancing Magpie club

TAMARA – barmaid at the Dancing Magpie

MEL TOOMEY – restaurant owner

GERRY DUNNE – doorman at the Montague club

FABIO – barman at the Montague club

# DAY ONE

Monday, 28 March 1983

# ONE

The vision of blood streaming down his shirt hit Matt at unexpected moments. This time the trigger was the door in the outer office creaking as it swung open. He put the tape recorder down, unbuttoned his shirt and peered down at his chest. He knew of course that it was only in his head, but the pictures in his mind were sometimes so real he had to check. No stream of red, just an ugly purple scar. A reminder of the day his world collapsed, and the light went out on his glittering career.

Now there were voices next door. His cat, sleeping on the warm window ledge as usual, opened his eyes and languidly stretched out a paw. Matt looked up towards the frosted glass door, engraved in bold lettering with "M.G. CRAWFORD". Dark shapes were moving in the outer office and his assistant Kate's typewriter stopped with a ding. There was a woman's voice he didn't recognise. Kate answered her in a soothing tone. He knew Kate would usher her to a seat and offer her a glass of water. He relaxed when he heard the liquid pouring. Matt guessed he had a few minutes while Kate extracted the basic details. She was an expert in filtering out the time-wasters. He composed himself and started the recorder. Speaking softly, he scanned a series of glossy black-and-white prints spread across his desk. A young woman was welcoming an older man at her front door, wearing little more than a big grin and heavy make-up.

'The enclosed photos show your husband entering the house in question at 6.15pm on the evening of—'

At that moment the phone rang. He pressed the pause button, put the recorder down and reached over to pick up the receiver. It was Kate. 'Can I pop in a moment?'

'Sure, just give me two minutes.'

He left his chair, stood in front of the mirror and ran a comb through his thick, ruffled hair. Then his curiosity got the better of him. He walked towards the door and opened it a few inches. At the far side of the main office, he saw Kate talking to a young woman, who was sitting hunched up on the edge of the leather sofa. She looked very bohemian in flared blue jeans, with dark curls falling over a floaty purple blouse. Kate, continuing to speak to her in soft tones, saw Matt peeking through the door. 'Can you excuse me for a moment, Mrs Mackie?'

Kate picked up an envelope from her desk and crossed the room to Matt's office, closing the door behind her. Matt was sitting on the edge of the desk while Kate remained standing, her hand still on the doorknob.

'What's the story?' he said.

'Mrs Mackie. Missing husband.' Matt raised an eyebrow. 'Five days.'

'Has she been to the police?'

'Yes, she has, but they're not taking it seriously.'

'Really? Now there's a thing,' said Matt, trying to keep the boredom out of his voice. Another domestic was looming. He stroked the stubble on his chin. 'Well, I'm not sure we can help either.'

Kate waved the envelope in front of his face. 'This landed on my desk this morning. Know what it is? Our landlord's final rent demand.'

Matt looked more interested now. 'How did she…?'

'A friend of hers recommended you, Fiona Campbell? West Bridgford florist,' said Kate. 'Her ex, Philip, is a lecturer at the university, specialising in foreign students with long legs and limited means.'

He smiled at the memory. 'Fabulous Fiona.'

'Now happily divorced with most of her husband's income,' muttered Kate.

'I aim to please,' said Matt, stifling a yawn. He'd had a late night, waiting for an adulterous wife to appear from a swanky Edwardian house in a well-to-do Nottingham suburb.

Hands on hips, Kate stared him down. 'So?'

'Ask Mrs Mackie to come through.'

Sitting opposite him, Mrs Mackie pulled at the beaded necklace which dangled over her blouse. 'I want you to find my husband Steve. He's disappeared.'

'Disappeared or taken a break?'

'Disappeared.'

'Any reason why he might do that? An argument about something? Money?'

'No. I leave that side of things to him. It's easier that way. He's the one with the business brain.'

'How long have you been married?'

'It will be four years next month.'

'Maybe he just needed time away.'

She twisted her wedding ring around her finger. 'Steve wouldn't just up and leave without telling me. Something has happened to him, and I want you to find out what.'

Matt smacked his lips and leant back in his seat. 'Do you want my advice, Mrs Mackie? Save your money; go home; get some sleep; and let the police take care of things. I've been in this game a while. Fifteen years in the force and two years here. Long enough to know that the odds are he'll probably come back under his own steam.'

Her face reddened. She shuffled in her seat and straightened her back. 'Fiona said you were a private investigator. Are you, or aren't you? Because the police aren't interested so, if you won't help me, I'll walk the streets on my own, until I find him.'

He was strumming his fingers on the desk while he thought. When he stopped, he gave a sigh, opened a drawer and pulled out a notebook. 'Okay, so when did you see him last?'

'Wednesday morning. I dropped him off at work as usual at 8am.'

'Where's that?'

'At his office in West Bridgford. On Rectory Road.'

He made a note with a biro. 'He doesn't drive?'

6

'He's serving a ban, so it's either me or a taxi for getting around.'

'Likes a drink, does he?'

'His work is stressful. Steve set up his own estate agency a year ago. It's been a hard slog.'

'I'll need a recent photo.'

She picked up her blue paisley handbag from the floor and undid the zip. From her purse she pulled out a Polaroid photo and handed it to Matt. 'That's my Steve. I took it on holiday last summer, in Menorca, on his thirtieth birthday.'

Matt scrutinised the photo. Steve Mackie was sitting at a beach bar wearing swimming shorts and a multicoloured shirt with a palm tree pattern. He was squinting in the sunlight and holding up a bottle of San Miguel. His steely eyes and cleft chin reminded Matt of Kirk Douglas. When he and his brother Richard were teenagers, his mum had dragged the whole family out to watch *Spartacus* at the Savoy.

'You last saw him on Wednesday. What was his mood?'

She looked down at the floor, slowly shaking her head. 'Quiet. I think he'd had a bad day on Tuesday. He got home about 8pm and, by the smell on his breath, he'd had a few. He'd phoned me at the office earlier to say he had a couple of evening viewings, but my guess is that the only house he'd entered was a public one.'

'Does he often stay out late?'

She took a few seconds to reply. 'It comes with the job. Steve belongs to a club in town and sometimes meets business contacts there – the Montague club.'

'The Montague? I've never been in, but I know it. No entrance without a jacket and tie.'

'Steve thinks it's important to move in the right circles.'

'So, when he didn't come home on Wednesday night?'

'I phoned everyone I could think of on Thursday morning. His office, his best friends, his mum and dad and his sister. Nothing. I know he met up with a friend for lunch on Wednesday. His secretary told me he'd had two appointments with clients in the afternoon but failed to show. He never does that.'

'Has your husband ever stayed out overnight before and not told you?'

'No, never,' she said.

'Did you notice if any of his clothes were gone, or maybe if he'd packed a bag?'

'As far as I could see he hadn't taken anything from his wardrobe and both our suitcases are still in the cupboard. That's why I'm so…' she faltered, as if something had flashed across her mind, '…concerned.'

'What is it?'

'I've just remembered something.'

'Well?'

'There was a phone call recently. It was early evening and Steve wasn't back from work. It was a man's voice on the line, and I didn't recognise it. When I told him Steve wasn't there, he seemed very annoyed. Then when I asked him who was calling, he put the receiver down.'

'When was this?'

'No more than two weeks ago.'

'Try to remember exactly. Can you recall what you were doing when the phone rang?'

She pursed her lips. 'I was watching the news. It was

Geoffrey bloody Howe announcing that the tax on wine had gone up five pence a glass.'

'Budget day.' Matt made a note. 'That helps. Did you mention the call to Steve?'

'Yes. He said it was probably one of his mates.'

'But you didn't believe him.'

She fixed her deep brown eyes to his. Matt noticed her long dark eyelashes were natural. 'No, I didn't; he was biting his bottom lip. He only does that when he's lying. Besides, the man on the phone had a Geordie accent. None of Steve's friends come from the north-east as far as I'm aware.' She took a tissue from her pocket and dabbed her nose and eyes.

'Are you okay? We can break now, if you like?'

His unexpected concern softened the tension in her face. 'No, it's nothing, I'm just tired really.'

'If you're sure, then…'

'I'm quite sure,' said Mrs Mackie, pocketing her tissue.

'When did you and your husband first meet?'

'Seven years ago. I'd found my first job and was looking for a flat to rent. Steve did the viewing. A week later he called and invited me out for a drink.'

'Estate agent privileges, eh?'

'I suppose.'

'Do you have any children?'

'No. We both have very demanding jobs.' She paused for a brief sigh. 'I'm a solicitor, with Brown, McAuley and Partners. I deal with wills and probate.'

'The office on The Ropewalk?' said Matt.

'Yes, that's right. Suppose you think my job's pretty mundane? It can be at times, but it pays well.' She leaned towards him. 'Will you find my husband?'

'I'll make a few enquiries.'

'Your assistant didn't mention money.'

'I won't lie to you about this kind of case, Mrs Mackie,' said Matt.

'Hazel,' said Mrs Mackie.

'Tracing your husband, Hazel, might take a day, or I could spend weeks looking for him with no guarantee of success. Most disappearances are voluntary, and some people just walk out on their lives for good without notice. If he had been attacked, he would most likely have been found by now or have been admitted to hospital. If you want me to go ahead, my rate is £25 an hour, plus expenses.'

'Whatever it takes. I just want you to find him.'

'I'll have my assistant draw up a contract. I'll need a list of all his close friends, family and staff at the agency, with addresses and phone numbers if you have them?'

She took a folded piece of paper from her bag and handed it to him. 'I wrote all the information I could think of on here.'

He opened it and studied the scribbled list. 'Who did Steve meet up with last Wednesday?'

'Harry Barton. His details are there.'

He traced his finger down the page and gave a nod. 'Good. I think I have enough for now. Let's see what Kate and Desmond are up to, shall we?'

'Desmond?'

'The cat. Named him after Desmond Dekker.'

She frowned. 'Who?'

'The reggae singer; his backing group is called The Aces. Do you know "Israelites" and "007"?'

'Can't say that I do. Fancy yourself as James Bond then?'

He gave her a wry smile. 'Not anymore. All those years in the force knocked it out of me, I think.'

Matt got up from his chair and ushered Hazel through the door. Kate was sitting at her desk and the cat was rubbing himself against her leg. On the desk stood an empty plate with remnants of chocolate cake. She saw him pointing at the corner of his mouth as he approached behind Mrs Mackie. Kate smiled and slowly licked the offending crumb away from the corner of her mouth. Two sets of contracts had already been laid out next to her typewriter, waiting for signature. Matt signed both copies and then handed them to his new client. Hazel studied them in silence for a few minutes, took a pen from Kate and signed on the dotted line.

'When can I expect to hear from you?' asked Hazel as Matt led her to the door.

'As soon as I have something to report I'll be in touch. Try and get some rest if you can.'

The office door closed behind her and a few seconds later Matt peered out of the front window to see her walking back along the pavement to her car. 'What do you think about our Mrs Mackie?' he asked.

'I think she's nice, but not in the same way that you do.'

'Bloody hell, am I that obvious?'

'I know you, Matt Crawford.'

'And I know you, Kate Brooks,' he said, looking pointedly at the plate. 'Miss breakfast again, did we? What do you make of her story? Do you believe it?'

She raised her eyebrows. 'Don't *you*?'

'Something doesn't feel right. If she really is so worried about her husband going missing, why did she leave it until the next morning to start calling people?'

# DAY TWO

Tuesday, 29 March 1983

# TWO

Matt parked his light blue VW Beetle near a playing field on the edge of West Bridgford, where roads sprawled out like the spokes of a wheel south of the river Trent. He got out of his car and walked past a football pitch with rusting goalposts and a sports pavilion with ugly graffiti scrawled across its rotting wooden walls. He pulled out his notepad to check the house number, then crossed the road to a double-fronted bungalow. Entering via a wooden gate, he headed along a slabbed path to the front door. Soon after he rang the bell, the door opened and a tall young woman appeared, squinting into the morning sun.

'Mrs Barton? I'm here to see your husband.'

The woman held her hand below her blonde fringe and eyed him from head to toe. 'Mr Crawford?'

'Yes. Is everything okay?'

'Sorry, yes. I had a picture of someone older when we spoke last night.'

'Let me guess. Was he wearing a beige raincoat and a Trilby hat?'

She blushed. 'Won't you come in?' She stepped back from the doorway to allow him into the porch and gestured in the direction of a half-open door at the end of the hall. 'Harry is waiting for you in the lounge. Some tea?'

'Kind of you. Just a hint of milk and no sugar.'

Matt's leather soles clomped loudly on the parquet floor as he strode past a very orderly coat stand and a potted rubber plant with highly polished dark green leaves. As he got closer, he took in the sweet smell of burning wood. He gave a knock before entering. A rotund, full-bearded man with long and scruffy brown hair was sitting in a wheelchair close to the fireplace. He wore a green tartan dressing gown which was straining to cover the pyjamas he wore underneath. The kindling wood was crackling, and the coal was beginning to smoke. Matt's eyes were taken by a silver-framed photograph on the mantelpiece above. The little family group were huddled together in a back garden. Sandwiched between a clean-shaven Harry and his blonde wife was a little girl in school uniform with a satchel over her shoulder.

Harry spoke with a soft and trembling voice, as if his vocal cords were fragile. 'Mr Crawford, I presume. Please take a seat.' He gestured to an armchair in the corner. As he did so, Matt noticed how delicate his fingers were, in contrast to the rest of his bulky frame. 'I hear Hazel has hired you to find Steve?'

'I'm making a few enquiries about his disappearance,'

said Matt, pulling out his notepad and pen. 'You had lunch with him on Wednesday, I hear?'

'Yes, that's right.'

'Where was that?'

'At the Test Match pub in West Bridgford.'

'I know it. The place next to the chippy on the main road into town. Looks like an old cinema inside.'

'Not a beer drinker's pub, but Steve likes it.'

'How long have you two been friends?'

Harry stroked his beard. 'Must be nearly ten years now.'

'How did you guys meet?'

'We belong to the same rowing club.'

'Which one?'

'The Water's Edge, on the embankment close to Trent Bridge. That's where we all…'

At that moment the door swung open, and Linda Barton came in with a tray of tea. 'Talking about me behind my back again?' she said with a stiff smile, then put the tray down on the table and began to pour. She placed Harry's mug of tea on the tray attached to his wheelchair, before passing Matt his drink.

'I was just telling Mr Crawford how we met,' said Harry.

'Still a keen rower, Mrs Barton?' asked Matt.

Linda sat on the edge of her chair, cradling her drink in both hands. 'As a matter of fact, yes. But I'm guessing you didn't come here to talk about that. How can we help, Mr Crawford?'

Matt turned to Harry. 'How was Steve when you saw him on Wednesday?'

Harry scratched his neck. 'A bit nervous.'

'What made you think that?' asked Matt.

'He kept looking around the bar. Like he was expecting to see someone.'

'What did you talk about?'

'He told me about his plans for the business. Then he asked if I could help him.'

'What sort of help?' asked Matt.

Harry hesitated and glanced over at his wife. 'He needed a loan.'

'How much?'

Harry coughed. The fumes from the fire were irritating his throat. '£1000.'

Matt took a note. 'A grand; did he tell you why he needed it?'

'No.'

'And you didn't ask?'

Harry shook his head. 'Didn't need to. Told him straight I couldn't help.'

'Has he ever asked you for money before?' asked Matt.

'Never.'

'What did he say when you turned him down?'

'He tried to talk me round. Told me it was just for a couple of weeks.'

'But you didn't believe him?' said Matt.

Harry frowned. 'It's not that. I don't have that sort of cash to lend to anyone.'

'Did you mention anything about this to Mrs Mackie when she called?' asked Matt.

Harry looked over at Linda again. She was slowly shaking her head. 'I thought it best not to,' he said.

Matt paused to take a slurp of tea and smacked his lips; a bit too much milk for his liking. 'How are things between them?'

'Don't see too much of them these days, but they seem happy enough,' said Harry.

'You used to be closer?' said Matt.

There was an uncomfortable silence. Harry looked down at his legs. Linda turned to Matt. 'Before the accident, yes.'

'The accident?' said Matt.

'A car crash. Harry was lucky to survive,' said Linda, with a nod towards her husband.

'When was this?' asked Matt.

Linda shuffled on the settee. 'Two years ago,' she said. 'It was all over the papers. Harry's friend Carl Price was killed.'

'I think I remember it now,' said Matt. 'Were you on a stag night?'

'That's right; Carl was getting married,' said Harry, letting out a heavy sigh.

'Were you at the wheel, Mr Barton?'

Harry cleared his throat. 'No. Carl was driving,' he said, his eyes moistening. 'It was three days before his wedding. Steve Mackie was the other passenger.'

'Was he hurt too?' asked Matt.

'A gashed leg and bruised ribs. He's always been the lucky one.'

'Getting back to Wednesday. When did you leave the pub?'

'Linda came to pick me up at about 2pm.'

'And what about Steve?'

'He'd headed off in a taxi a few minutes earlier, leaving me to pick up the tab.'

'Do you know whose taxi it was?'

'No. The barman made the call.'

'Did he mention where he was going?'

'No, but he said he had a meeting to get to.'

Matt looked down at his notebook. 'Do you know if Steve has a Geordie friend, from the rowing club, maybe?'

Harry stroked his beard, then shook his head. 'No one comes to mind.'

'Give me a call if you think of anyone,' said Matt, leaning forwards and placing his business card on the table. 'There is just one more thing before I go. Can you think of anywhere your friend might be? A special place he likes to go to?'

'Nowhere specific. Steve's the outdoor type; he likes water and the sun, the beach and the river.'

Trying not to think about how many hundreds of beaches and rivers there were in England alone, Matt closed his notebook up, pocketed his pen and got to his feet. He pointed towards the mantelpiece. 'A pretty girl, your daughter.'

Harry's eyes gleamed for the first time as he looked across the room at the photograph. 'That was Zoe's first day at grammar school, four years ago,' he said, colour flooding to his cheeks. 'She's as bright as a button. Gets that from her mum.'

\*\*\*

Back at the office, Kate was thumbing through a card index file next to her phone.

'Any joy from the morgues?' asked Matt, with a wry grin.

She sniggered. 'No, he's not turned up so far.'

'What about the hospitals?'

'No luck there either I'm afraid, but I'll keep going down the list. How did it go on bread and lard island?'

'Where?'

'That's what the locals call West Bridgford. The story goes that the people who live there spend so much money on the mortgage and fur coats that it's all they can afford to eat.'

He laughed. 'Haven't heard that one before, although I can think of a few that fit that description. But not Harry and Linda Barton.'

'What are they like, then?'

Matt rubbed the back of his neck. 'Put on a good show for me, but I sensed a tension between them. Do you remember that fatal car crash in Bramcote a couple of years back? Driver hit a tree?'

'How could I forget it? My pig-headed boss at the *Post* gave the story to his blue-eyed boy, Keith Ferrell. And not long after that, I gave him my resignation letter.'

Matt held his arms out wide. 'And look at you now, transformation from local reporter to private snoop complete.'

She brushed a stray strand of auburn hair away from her freckled face and crinkled her nose. 'Never have much luck with bosses, do I?' She didn't mean it, and he knew that too. They'd first met three years ago. Matt was just out of hospital and Kate had come to interview him at home. He and Amanda were still together then. His chest was heavily bandaged, and his stitches pulled with every slight body movement. The young woman the *Evening Post* had sent to interview him had shown more insight and compassion than any other journalist he'd met in his police career. He must have made an impression on her too. Eighteen months later, he'd been happily surprised to find her application amongst the pile of responses to his job advert.

'Anyway, boss, *what* about the accident?' she asked.

'Harry Barton was badly injured in the crash. He was one of two passengers. Can you guess the other one's name?'

'Steve Mackie?'

'Correct. Harry can only get around on wheels now. If you recall, the driver, Carl Price, was killed.'

Kate pursed her lips. 'You think this might be relevant?'

'I'd say it's a valid line of inquiry. Maybe you can give your old buddy Keith Ferret a ring and see what he remembers about it?'

'It's Ferrell, with two l's, not Ferret! Suppose he is a bit rodent-like, now I come to think—'

'Whatever, just call him, will you?' Matt sighed, pulled out his notebook and scrutinised the list he'd made. 'When you've done that, can you call the Test Match pub in West Bridgford to find out which taxi firm they use? Steve met Harry there the day he went missing. He left in a cab just before 2pm.'

She made notes on an A4 pad in beautifully neat, curly handwriting and looked up in expectation of more, but nothing came. 'What did you make of Harry Barton?'

He tapped his pen on the desk. 'You mean do I trust him? I don't know. Do I think he knows more than he told me? Almost certainly. Maybe I need to catch him another time when his wife Linda's not at home.'

# THREE

By early afternoon the sun had done a disappearing act as Matt drove south of the city along London Road in a heavy shower. He passed the sprawling, red-brick railway station on his right before grinding to a halt. He crawled towards Trent Bridge, his windscreen wipers clearing the blur of the raindrops to reveal a stationary line of cars ahead. Looking to his left along the river, he saw two rowing crews heading downstream on rippling, silvery water. They were moving a lot faster than his old VW Beetle, its engine ticking like some giant sewing machine. It had been built with German precision of course, but it didn't purr like his brother Richard's new six-cylinder BMW, and it had rust bubbles over the back bumper.

The queue thinned out as Matt turned left into Bridgford Road and, passing behind the tall-chimneyed pavilion at Trent Bridge cricket ground, headed for West

Bridgford town centre. Steve Mackie's secretary, Monica Purvis, had given him directions over the phone. The offices of Mackie Estates occupied the ground floor of a large, terraced house amongst a small line of shops opposite the fire station. Not a prime High Street location, but close enough to attract passing foot traffic. A banner across the top of the front window bore the slogan "LOOK NO FURTHER!" in large red letters. As Matt came through the door, Monica was just finishing a call. He recognised the lilt of her Scottish accent from their telephone call. The secretary puffed out her cheeks and peered at him through tiny eyes over silver half-moon glasses. He was put in mind of one of the hamsters he'd kept as a boy.

'Can I help at all?' she asked.

'Matt Crawford. We spoke earlier.'

'Yes, of course.' She gestured towards a chair. 'Please take a seat for a moment. I'll get my colleague to take over from me.'

She got up from her desk and called her young assistant who emerged from what looked like a small kitchen at the back of the office. The gangly, ginger-haired girl looked barely out of school. The secretary then asked Matt to follow her through to a back room, separated by a half-glazed partition from the rest of the office. Unlike the outer office, it was carpeted, and on the polished oak desk stood a stainless steel name plaque bearing Steve Mackie's name. Next to it, on a side table, he noticed the very latest blue push-button Trimphone complete with answering machine. Monica showed him to a fake leather seat which squeaked as Matt sat down. She sat opposite him, leaving her boss's high-backed executive chair behind the desk vacant.

Monica straightened up her jacket as Matt began to speak.

'When was it you last saw Mr Mackie?' he asked.

'Last Wednesday afternoon, as he was leaving for lunch.'

'What time was that?'

'It was about fifteen minutes before my lunch break. So, I'd say around 12.15pm.'

Matt jotted this down on his notepad. 'During the morning, how did he seem to you?'

She paused to scratch her forehead. 'I had a feeling something was bothering him.'

'Business problems?'

'He didn't say.'

'What made you think something wasn't right?'

'He looked strangely vacant when he came in. Then he was chain-drinking filter coffee all morning.'

Matt fidgeted with his ballpoint pen. 'Do you have any idea what was bothering Steve?'

She pushed her bottom lip out. 'Not really. He's been very busy these past few weeks, though. We're involved in a new housing scheme over in Stapleford and it's taking up most of his time.'

Matt paused to thumb back a few pages in his notebook. 'I see from my notes that Steve had two appointments that afternoon.'

'Yes, that's right.'

'Can I see the details?' asked Matt.

Monica sprang up, went over to the desk and came back with a leather-bound diary. Back in her seat, she quickly located the page and ran her forefinger down it. 'He had two accompanied viewings. The first was in Beeston at 3pm with a Mr Henson. The second one was back here in West Bridgford at 4.30pm with Mr and Mrs Judd.'

'And he didn't make either?'

Monica pulled her glasses down her nose and rubbed her eyes. 'No, he didn't. I got a torrent of abuse over the phone from Mr Henson. Said he'd waited twenty minutes and then given up.'

'And the other clients?'

'I found their message on the answering machine on Thursday morning. I'd only just finished listening to it when Mrs Mackie called.'

'Had you already tried to phone her?'

Monica's jaw stiffened. 'No, I hadn't. I feel bad about that now. The thing is, Steve is not always the most reliable, so I wasn't overly concerned.'

'I'll need the addresses for both properties and the phone numbers of the vendors. Plus, the contact details for Mr Henson and the er...'

'Judds,' she said, jogging his memory. 'I'll get them for you in a moment. There is just one more thing. On Thursday morning, I found a second message.'

Matt leant towards her. 'What about it?'

'It was a woman's voice. She seemed to know Steve quite well.'

'I'd like to hear it if you've still got it,' he said. 'Please tell me you haven't erased it?'

'No, I haven't, I thought it best to keep them.' She walked over to the side table and pressed the play button on the silver box next to the phone. After winding it forward twice she found the message she was seeking. The woman spoke with a Welsh accent and there was tension in her voice. 'Steve, it's me… we need to talk. Call me when you get this message.'

Matt looked thoughtful. 'Is her voice familiar? Is it one of his family, a close friend, perhaps?'

'I don't think so.'

He narrowed his eyes. 'You don't think so. Are you sure?'

Monica nodded. 'I am, yes.'

'Then I'll need to take the tape with me.'

'I don't know if Steve would…'

'It might help us find him.'

'But now you've heard it surely…'

'Do I have to get Mrs Mackie to come here herself because you won't co-operate? Don't think she'll be best pleased, do you?'

Monica sighed. 'I suppose it's okay then.' She reluctantly pressed the eject button, pulled out the cassette and gave it to him. He quickly slipped it into his inside jacket pocket.

'Now, was there anything more?' she asked. 'I don't like leaving my assistant out front on her own.'

'Won't keep you much longer, but I need you to tell me a little more about Mr Mackie. What is he like as a boss?'

She stared across at the empty executive chair. 'He's easy enough to get on with and clients like him. He has his moods, but that comes with the stress of the job. I've known him long enough now to—'

'How long have you worked here?'

'Since we opened at the start of last year. Steve and I worked together at Harlow's Estate Agents for two years before that. They're just around the corner on Central Avenue. Our old boss thought Steve was a walking disaster. It's true he can be a wee bit disorganised, but that's where I come in.'

'What made you leave Harlow's?'

She crossed her arms. 'Steve mainly. And the chance of a fresh start. I'd been there too long.'

Matt was getting the picture. 'And Mackie Estates, has it been a success?'

She pointed through the window to wall-to-ceiling notice boards in the main office which were plastered with laminated property photos. 'As you see, there's no lack of houses to sell. Problem is, they are not moving very fast. Steve blames the recession. Says we just need to ride it out.'

Monica paused and looked across to a large pine-framed photograph on the wall behind the desk. In the grainy colour enlargement, the petite Monica just about reached the shoulders of her smiling boss. They were standing close together in front of their office. She was dressed in a smart trouser suit and Steve was wearing a double-breasted navy-blue blazer and a pink and green floral tie. 'I do hope he's not in any—'

She was interrupted by the high-pitched trilling of the phone. She reached over the desk and picked up. 'Who's calling? Brooks… for Mr Crawford. Yes, he's here with me. I'll pass you over.'

Matt, already on his feet, took the phone from Monica and held it to his ear. 'Kate? You have news?'

There was a breathless excitement in her voice. 'I've tracked down the taxi that picked Steve Mackie up from the pub. The driver remembered Steve from the description I gave him. Says he took him to an address in Beeston.'

'Where exactly?'

'Tells me he dropped him at a house on Meadow Road.' Matt looked across at Monica, who was listening intently. She confirmed with a nod.

'Did he give you a time?'

'He thinks it was around 2.30pm.'

*Half an hour before he was due to meet his client there*, thought Matt. *So why hadn't he shown up?*

# FOUR

Darkness was beginning to fall when Matt pulled into a parking space behind the office building. It wasn't an ideal situation, living and working in the same building, but he'd had no wish to stay in the marital home. In contrast, after their divorce, his ex-wife Amanda had been happy to remain in the semi-detached nest they had decorated and furnished to her taste. It had thick-pile fitted carpets, designer wallpaper, Scandinavian furniture and drapes over the bed. He guessed it was the sort of decor that his ex-wife's new boyfriend, Guy Travers, would appreciate. Matt suspected that Amanda spent most of her time at Guy's house; actually, it was more of a mansion than a house. Matt tried to tell himself that he was not envious. He wanted to believe that he was happy in his one-bedroomed flat with threadbare carpets and manky net curtains. And, after all, she *had* let him take the cat.

As he got out of the car, he was glad to see Kate's Mini still there. Matt was glad he had found someone equally dedicated to detective work. He walked around the back of the ancient two-storey building and through an archway onto the street. The ornate Victorian buildings that came into view along the main street housed legal practices, insurance companies, private health clinics, financial advisors and accountants. His thoughts turned back to Guy Travers, who ran his own accountancy firm. Guy wore hand-stitched suits and carried a real leather briefcase. Matt guessed that Guy spent more of his time worrying about the guest list for his next dinner party than his clients' welfare. It made him feel nauseous.

Matt sidled a little wearily through the front door; last night's surveillance was beginning to catch up with him. What made it worse was that his target, a prominent local politician, was proving slippery. After several hours of fruitless observation from his car, Matt had driven despondently back through Nottingham in the early hours, just as the nightclub revellers were spilling onto the streets. As he was thumping the steering wheel to the beat of "Tainted Love", two young girls in miniskirts and high heels had stood in the road and waved down his car. He had wound down the window and informed them that he was not a taxi. Times like these made him wish he was back in the force. He knew that serious injury and trauma prevented this, but it didn't stop him thinking it.

At the end of the hallway, he pushed open the office door to find Kate, headphones on, transcribing his latest dictation. She stopped typing and eyed him from head to toe, as if checking he was all there.

'Look what the cat brought in,' she said, a twinkle of mischief in her green eyes.

He chuckled. 'Very funny. Where is Desmond, by the way?'

'Chasing mice in the back garden. He was miaowing at the back door, so I let him out.'

'You didn't need to stay on, you know?'

She looked down at a stack of paperwork on her desk. 'I had to catch up with some filing. And I wanted to update you.'

'Sounds promising,' he said, pulling up a chair next to her desk. 'What have you got for me?'

'I've spoken to Keith Ferrell at the *Evening Post*. As it turned out, he remembered the accident well. He told me that Carl Price, the driver, had more than twice the legal alcohol limit in his blood. There was no other vehicle involved. Keith got an interview with Carl's mother soon after the tragedy; her name's Ellie Price. She told him that Carl was an only child and that she'd brought him up on her own. Her son was a sensible lad, with a good job in teaching. She couldn't understand why he'd done something so stupid.'

'Umm… my mum used to think I was an angel too. She knows better now. Did Keith Ferrell interview Steve Mackie at the time?'

'I asked him about that. Apparently, Steve turned him down and Harry Barton was too sick to speak to anyone.'

'Does he know about Steve going missing?'

'No, but as soon as I told him, he couldn't wait to get off the phone. My guess is he ran straight to Mr Oink with it.'

'Who?'

'Mr Oink, my old boss at the *Evening Post*. He with the pig-like head… well, maybe not. That's an insult to such intelligent animals.'

'Not a big fan of his, are you? I'll be interested to see what they make of the story. How about Carl's Price's fiancée? She's sure to know Steve. Did Keith mention her at all?'

'No, he didn't. Maybe I should have—'

'Give him another call and see if he knows who she is. Let's keep in touch with him and see what he digs up. Maybe you could have lunch with him? On expenses of course.'

'Don't know if I could survive a whole lunch with Keith; we could meet up for a coffee I guess.'

'And cakes.'

She grinned. 'Well, if it's on expenses… anyway enough of Keith, I'm curious to know how it went this afternoon.'

'Steve's secretary seems smitten. Didn't have a bad word to say about him. She gave me the rundown on the two viewings he missed. Oh… and I got this too.' He pulled out the cassette from his jacket pocket and handed it to her. 'This message was left on Steve Mackie's answering machine the day he disappeared. Give it a play and tell me what you think.'

Kate ejected the cassette she had been using and replaced it with the answering machine tape. Matt got her to wind it back to the start of the woman's message. His assistant listened intently through her headphones, then stopped the tape and pulled them off. She brushed her hair back into place with her fingers and was quiet for a few seconds. Matt gave her the look of a schoolmaster waiting for a pupil to respond.

'She's Welsh,' said Kate.

'I'd got that far myself,' he said, with a sarcastic grin.

'And she's agitated, angry with him.'

'Yes... good.'

'She's a close friend, or maybe family?'

'Excellent. So now I'd like you to ring Hazel Mackie and ask her to drop in tomorrow. Maybe she can identify this lady. And there is something else as well.' He got to his feet, took out a folded piece of paper from his back pocket and gave it to her. 'Here are the numbers of the two clients Steve didn't show up for. I'd like you to call them. Find out exactly how and why they made the appointment and what happened on that day.'

'You think they may be somehow involved?'

'Probably not, but we can at least eliminate them from our inquiries. Let's see what they have to say, shall we?'


Matt saw Kate to the front door. She was unaware of him watching her as she made her way along the front of the building; her skirt swaying as she turned into the car park. He walked heavy footed back into the office, where the scent of her perfume still hung in the air. Matt took a bunch of keys from his desk drawer and went through the ritual of locking all the doors. *Wonder what Kate has planned for tonight? A dinner party with friends or the Playhouse theatre maybe?* It was the loneliest part of his day. The building was quiet; the office cleaners had long since gone home. The streets outside were dark and deserted and his life seemed to be the same. He felt irritated by his own inertia. There were things he needed to say, feelings he wanted to share. But he couldn't bring himself to do it. Not yet.

Outside in the main corridor, he turned left and another twenty paces took him to the door of his flat. Its shiny black paint and polished brass knocker gave a false impression of what lay inside. He fumbled for his keys and unlocked it, switching the lights on as he entered the tiny hallway. Then he took off his jacket and hung it on a metal coat hook on the wall. Entering the kitchen, he winced as he took in the smell of sour milk from his unwashed breakfast bowl.

He took a tin of baked beans from the cupboard and attacked it with a can opener. He poured the contents into a waiting saucepan and lit the gas burner with a match. While that was heating, he pulled out a loaf from the bread bin, cut two slices and put them in the toaster. Then he opened the fridge for the butter, but there was none. Toast without butter was not the best, but he'd have to make do. He added "butter" to the shopping list attached by a magnet to the fridge door. Next to it was a holiday postcard from his brother Richard. It was a picture of gondolas in Venice. It served as a painful reminder of the gulf in lifestyle between them, which had widened since he was attacked. Until his stabbing, Matt had been on the fast track to promotion himself. Now his older brother had been appointed DCI and was not afraid to splash his money around. *Still, no bad thing to have someone I can trust in the force*, he thought. *If only he weren't so bloody good at his job.*

He ate quickly, wiped tomato sauce from his lips and added the plate and cutlery to the heap of dirty dishes in the sink. Washing up would have to wait. Matt glanced up at the kitchen clock. It was 8pm and he was running late; there was little time to shave, wash and dress. He'd decided to give himself a night off watching the canoodling councillor. Grateful as he was, there was a downside to what he'd planned for the evening. He was going to need a clean shirt, smart suit, polished shoes and, worst of all, a tie.

# FIVE

Sitting in the living room of her flat, Kate was beginning to wind down. She picked up an album from the shelf and slid the record out of the sleeve. She placed it on the turntable and moved the stylus carefully to the first track. It was one of her most-loved albums, *Tapestry*. The photo of Carole King on the album cover, sitting in a window, bare-footed and wearing jeans, reminded her of Hazel Mackie. She even had the same long, dark, wavy hair. Kate understood why Matt was attracted to Hazel; she had an effortless, natural beauty and seemed to be blissfully unaware of it. Kate had felt an affinity with her from the moment she'd come through their door and made her tearful appeal for help. Hazel was showing a brave face to the world whilst crumbling inside.

True, Matt had his doubts about Hazel, but then he was ex-police. She understood why he had an inbuilt suspicion of everyone. Not that she hadn't felt waves of cynicism during her years as a regional reporter. But Matt had come face to face with the worst of humanity; he'd been stabbed in the chest and come perilously close to death. When she'd interviewed him after he was attacked, he'd stuck rigidly to the facts. After an anonymous tip-off about a drugs deal, he'd gone into a house without backup and been savagely attacked. It was careless; he should have waited for his team to arrive. One mistake had changed his whole life, ruined his career. After a long period of recovery, Matt had put a suit of armour around his feelings, afraid that if they were exposed it would reveal a weakness. But they could not be contained forever; sooner or later he would have to open up about his trauma.

Kate picked up her glass from the coffee table and took a mouthful of Chardonnay. Her estranged husband, Luke, didn't share her taste in wine. Neither did his mistress apparently. It was almost two years to the day since Kate had come home unexpectedly early from a weekend training course. She'd found two wine glasses, one with an imprint of red lipstick, and an unfinished bottle of vintage Châteauneuf-du-Pape on the kitchen table. She'd heard a loud giggle coming from above and so crept slowly up the stairs to the bedroom. She caught Luke with his pants down and his partner covering her modesty with one of Kate's silk pillowcases. She recognised the woman from their tennis club: long blonde hair, a deep tan, posh accent, designer tennis gear and a bright pink headband. It was Glennis Dickens. One week later, still bubbling over inside from a mixture of anger and heartbreak, Kate had moved out to a friend's house. And a month after that she had found this place: a one-bedroomed second-floor flat overlooking the Trent.

Luke had let her have her choice of furniture from their home. Kate had taken a tall pine shelving unit to store her LPs and a matching bookcase to house her collection of paperbacks, mainly crime novels, as well as some philosophy text books from her university days: Jean-Paul Sartre, Heidegger and Kant. She'd had absolutely zero interest in taking the bed in which Luke had slept with his new lover. In fact, she'd needed to take a very deep breath to prevent herself from taking a saw to it before she left.

Kate sang along to her favourite track, "It's Too Late", then turned off the hi-fi. She picked up her glass and wandered out onto the small, iron-railed balcony. To her left, in the distance, she could see the outline of the two stone towers of the Wilford suspension bridge against the night sky. Their elaborate Edwardian carvings made them look like miniature versions of the Arc de Triomphe. Closer to her, she saw a couple walking arm in arm along the embankment. It reminded her of when she and Luke had first met. On weekends, they would stroll along that same path at night, the street lights reflecting from the river and silhouetting the trees. She had felt so at one with Luke then, so sure of his love for her... *Had Steve Mackie found someone else too?* she wondered. *Maybe they had run off together? They might even have left the country. Or was there another reason for his disappearance?*

The sudden ringing of the phone inside the flat interrupted her thoughts. She hurried through the balcony door, crossed the living room and headed to the phone, which hung from a wall in the hallway. She was surprised when she picked up the call; she had half expected another call from Luke, asking if she'd heard anything from her solicitors on the divorce.

'Hi, Kate, it's Keith. You left a message for me earlier. Is it about Steve Mackie?'

'Yes, it is.'

Kate could hear the clicking of typewriters in the background, telling her that her ex-colleague was still in the office at this late hour.

'The boss was chuffed we got the exclusive. Think I owe you one for that, Kate. What have you got for me?'

'Nothing new.' She detected his sigh of disappointment on the line. 'Something I forgot to ask you about the accident Steve was involved in. You told me it happened on Carl Price's stag night. Did you ever interview Carl's fiancée?'

'No, never had that pleasure, I'm afraid.'

'Remember her name?'

He paused for a few seconds. 'Diana… no, it was Diane… Diane Collins. I spoke to her mother who said that her daughter needed time and space to grieve. Diane chose not to talk to any of the media. To be honest, I don't think DS Collins trusted us.'

'Diane's a police officer?'

'Yes, she was at the time; no idea if she still is. Are you connecting her to Steve Mackie's disappearance?'

'Well, I'm guessing they know each other well. We're interested in everyone who is close to him.'

'Don't give me that flannel. Do you think he's involved with her?'

'I didn't say that, and I certainly don't have any reason to think it. We'd just like to have a word, that's all.'

He chuckled. 'You sound just like the police.'

'Do I really? You've been in touch with them, then?'

'Yes, but I was wasting my time. Spoke to the DI who's investigating. All he'd tell me was that they're doing all the usual checks. Hospitals, mortuaries, airports and so on. So far nothing.'

'What's the DI's name?' she asked.

'Joe Martin. The boss knows him; says he's a sound guy. I got the impression they're not allocating much manpower to your missing person case. Of course, they might be forced into action now that *we've* got hold of the story. By the way, it's made tomorrow's front page.'

# SIX

Right on cue, the rain began to fall soon after Matt began walking in the direction of the city centre. The nearer he got to the Old Market Square, the more intense the rainfall. Water was dripping from the two massive lion statues which stood at the front of the impressive, colonnaded Council House building as he made his way east in the direction of the Lace Market. He took cover near a shop window and checked his appearance in the reflection, if only to confirm that he was doing a brilliant impression of a water vole. He ran a comb through his spikey, sodden hair, brushed raindrops from the shoulders of his jacket and trudged on.

The Montague Club was halfway up a steepish hill on his right. It was a grey stone, three-storey early century building with ornate sash windows, which gave it an aura of opulence and privilege. He'd heard that it was *the* place to go in Nottingham, which was probably why he'd never darkened its doors until tonight. As he sloshed his way through puddles towards the front door, he got a glimpse of the restaurant, which was illuminated by a cluster of low-hanging crystal chandeliers.

He had barely reached the first step up to the door when a towering figure with close-cropped ginger hair emerged from the storm porch. The man had the build of a rugby forward and spoke in a husky tone. 'Good evening, sir. Could I trouble you for your member's card?'

Matt detected an Irish brogue in his voice. The bouncer loomed over him, blocking his path. Unruffled, the detective pulled his wallet from his inside jacket pocket. 'That won't be necessary. I'm here to meet one of your members… on business. Here's my card.' He didn't give him a card; he took out three ten-pound notes and slipped them discreetly into the big man's palm.

The doorman tucked the notes into his greatcoat pocket and stepped aside. As he did, Matt noticed his immaculate Doc Martin boots. 'The bar is to the right. Fabio will look after you. Tell him Gerry sent you and he'll see you're okay.'

The foyer had a diamond-patterned marble floor and flocked wallpaper. Gilt-framed portraits of unsmiling nobility hung on the walls. Their eyes seemed to follow Matt as he made his way through to the bar. Fabio, in dark suit and bow tie, was fastidiously wiping down the highly polished counter when Matt got there. The room was empty, save for a couple in the corner, who were too absorbed in one another and their champagne to notice him. Judging by the buzz of conversation and the plumes of pungent cigar smoke coming from the restaurant, most of the clientele were still having dinner. He guessed that, after they'd had their fill of French cuisine and fine wine, some of them might try their luck downstairs in the casino. Fabio looked up from his cleaning to see Matt approaching and hurriedly put his cloth down behind the bar.

'What can I get you, sir?'

Matt stood at the bar and cast his eye over the beer pumps. 'A pint of Guinness please. Gerry said you'd look after me.'

'I'll do my best.' The barman reached for a glass and held it up to the light. Satisfied it was sparking clean, he placed it under the nozzle, tilted it at forty-five degrees and pulled slowly on the tap handle. 'Will you be dining with us, sir?'

'No, don't like eating on my own.'

'Maybe this will help,' said Fabio, placing the glass with great care in front of the detective. Matt gave him a ten-pound note and told him to keep the change.

The detective took a healthy sip of the dark stuff and licked the creamy head from the side of his mouth. 'Look, I'll level with you,' he said, fixing Fabio in the eye. 'I came here to ask about someone.' Matt took his business card from his jacket gave it to the barman.

Fabio paused to read it. 'Who are you looking for?'

'His name's Steve Mackie. Know him?'

Fabio hesitated, then muttered, 'I'm not sure.'

Matt took the Polaroid snapshot that Hazel had given him from his jacket pocket and passed it over. 'Maybe this will jog your memory?'

The barman took it in both hands and studied it. He shrugged his shoulders and handed it back. 'Is he in some kind of trouble?'

'He's gone missing; his wife has hired me to find him.'

'I don't think…'

Matt gave him a hard stare. 'I know Steve Mackie was a regular of yours. Tell me, when did you last see him here?'

The barman rubbed the dark shadow of stubble on his chin. 'I haven't seen Mr Mackie for a while; I think it was about four weeks ago, maybe five.'

'Think hard. Can you remember the exact date?'

'I couldn't say for sure. We see so many customers here. I think it was at lunchtime during the week.'

Matt tilted his head. 'Was Mr Mackie with someone?'

'Yes, a lady.'

'His wife?'

'No, not Mrs Mackie. This lady was older.'

'Had you seen her with Steve Mackie before?'

'Not that I remember.'

'What was she like?'

'I remember her well; she was different. She was not overdressed like some of the ladies are for dining. She wore a smart trouser suit, and she wasn't wearing any make-up or fancy jewellery.'

'What else do you recall about her?'

Fabio blushed as a picture formed in his head. 'She had beautiful dark eyes and olive skin. She reminded me of a sweetheart I once had in Italy.'

'Was this a business meeting? Did it seem to you they were close friends?'

'I… I… really could not say.'

Matt fixed him in the eye. 'So, let me ask you this. Were they behaving like a couple?'

The barman adjusted his collar and cleared his throat. 'This is difficult. You see, all staff here have to behave with complete discretion, you understand?'

Matt smiled. 'Of course. And if anyone should ask me, you and I never spoke.'

Fabio's voice dropped to a whisper. 'The gentleman was holding the lady's hand across the table. They were gazing into each other's eyes.'

# DAY THREE

Wednesday, 30 March 1983

# SEVEN

Matt's whole body was trembling as he opened his eyes, only to find he was safe in his own bed, looking up at the familiar cracked ceiling. Although awake now and aware of his surroundings, the dream wouldn't let him go. The images still played in his painful, throbbing head: a snarling, pockmarked face, a muscled, tattooed arm, the glint of a blade caught by the light, a gaping chest wound with red lava-like liquid spilling from it. He'd cried out for help and, as he had done so, woke up from his nightmare, relieved not to be lying in a pool of his own blood. *It's just a dream, it's just a dream, it's just a dream...*

His hand still shaking, Matt reached over to his bedside table for the bottle of tablets. Sitting up in bed, he unscrewed the lid, took out two pills and put them into the palm of his hand. Then he washed them down with a gulp of water from the tumbler which he filled at bedtime every night. As he swallowed them, he wondered if the Prozac was actually making things worse, not better.

It was barely light outside, but he knew there was no point in trying to get more sleep while he was in such a heightened state. He brushed cold sweat from his cheeks and, as he got to his feet, he began to shiver. His dressing gown was draped over a nearby chair. Slipping it on over his pyjamas, he shuffled in the direction of the kitchen. Ignoring last night's washing-up, Matt put the kettle on and went in search of his notepad. He found it in his jacket, which was hanging on a peg in the hallway.

He threw his notebook down on the table on his way back to the kitchen. He made himself a strong coffee, sat down and, while he waited for it to cool, searched for a clean page. Having found one, he picked up his biro, steadied his hand and wrote a heading at the top of the sheet: *STEVE MACKIE*. Then he began scrawling some notes below it:

- *Guy with Geordie accent.*
- *Female voice on answerphone.*
- *Visit Meadow Road, neighbours?*
- *Speak to viewers: Mr Henson, Mr and Mrs Judd.*
- *Woman at the Montague club – who is she?*
- *Rowing club – Kate?*
- *Carl Price's fiancée.*

He drank half the mug of coffee in one gulp, then for a while sat in silence, staring down at the words, which flickered in and out of focus. He blinked sleep away from his eyes, took up his pen and started to write again: *Where would you go? With whom? Places, people. Family, friends and enemies. Who or what are you running from? Why?* And then finally, at the bottom, in large capitals, *WHERE THE HELL ARE YOU?*

\*\*\*

Two hours later, Matt found Kate already hard at work as he sidled slowly through the front office door. He approached her desk, leaning over her shoulder to take a look at what she was typing. It was his latest report on the errant councillor.

'Decided to give him a miss last night,' he said with a sigh. 'Went to Steve Mackie's fancy club instead.'

'Bet that was a treat. What was it like?'

'Much as I expected: full of trendy, rich people, wanting to be seen,' said Matt, as he circled the desk and took a seat opposite Kate. 'Made me want to throw up.'

'Didn't stop you staying late by the look of things,' said Kate, noticing the redness in his eyes.

'I just had the one drink. The whole place gave me the creeps. It was just like one of those gentleman's clubs you hear about in London. I don't know how the staff there put up with the arrogant members. Luckily for me, the barman was talkative enough once he found out I was not one of them. He told me our missing person recently had an intimate lunch with an older woman.'

'Do you think—'

'Steve's cheating on Hazel? There's a strong possibility.'

'Did he give you a name?'

'No, he said he hadn't seen her there before.'

'Are you going to say anything to Hazel?'

'Not until we know for sure. I don't want to rock the boat. She's got more than enough to cope with right now.'

Kate nodded in agreement. 'And there'll be more coming her way soon. Spoke to my old workmate Keith Ferrell from the *Evening Post* last night. Steve's disappearance will be in tonight's edition – front page.'

'Not a bad thing, I suppose. Maybe someone will read it and come forward.'

'Keith has already spoken to the police. The officer handling the case is DI Joe Martin.'

Matt's eyes widened. 'I know Joe. Our paths crossed once or twice. He's a reliable sort, but not the most dynamic. Must be getting close to his pension by now. What else did our friend the ferret give you?'

Kate stifled a grin. 'Stop calling him that. You don't even know him.'

'Now you're leaping to his defence. Are you sure you don't like him?'

'I'll ignore that last remark. Keith told me that Steve's late friend Carl Price was due to marry a police officer the day after the car crash. Her name's Diane Collins and she's a DS. I suppose you know her too?'

Matt noted the name on his pad and thought for a few seconds. 'No, but maybe my brother Richard can help there. That's a good start though.' He paused for a moment, then flicked back to the notes he'd written in the early hours, running his pen down the page.

'Any luck with the viewers Steve didn't show up for?' he asked.

'Yes. Got through to Mr Judd. His story tallied with what Steve's secretary had told you. Mr Judd and his wife waited around outside the house in West Bridgford for twenty minutes, then left a message with Steve's office.'

'What about Mr Henson from the house in Beeston? The one who gave them an earful when Steve didn't show?'

'Haven't been able to get an answer from Mr Henson, but I'll keep trying.'

'Good. Let me know if you have any luck. By the way, when is Hazel due to arrive?'

'In half an hour.'

He got up from his chair. 'It will be interesting to see what she makes of the answerphone message. Perhaps you could fire up the coffee machine in readiness? And do we have any biscuits that haven't gone soft?'

'Nothing but the best for Hazel, then?'

'She's a valued client,' he replied, a little too quickly.

She chuckled. 'We have plenty of those, but I don't see you offering *them* biscuits.'

He folded his arms. 'Are you going to make us coffee or what?'

# EIGHT

Forty minutes later, a breathless Hazel arrived and spluttered her apology for being late. Kate ushered her to a chair on the other side of her desk and gave Matt a ring to let him know. While she did so, Hazel was fidgeting in her seat and running her hand through her dark curls. She gladly accepted Kate's offer of coffee, although Kate wondered if the strong brew would only leave her overstimulated.

Soon after, Matt's door opened and he began to walk towards them, notebook in hand. Sensing that Desmond the cat was tailing him, Matt turned and shooed him back into his office, shutting the door. He greeted Hazel with a polite handshake and sat down opposite her.

'Are you okay?' he asked, leaning forwards in his chair.

Hazel looked up at the wall clock. 'I didn't get to sleep until the early hours. Then, at just after 7am, the phone rang. I rushed downstairs to answer it, thinking it might be Steve. Turned out it was a bloody newspaper reporter. I'm afraid I got upset and slammed the phone down on him.'

'I'm sorry,' said Matt, glancing over at Kate, 'we should have prepared you for that.'

'Then, just as I was leaving for the office, the post arrived. There was a letter, addressed to Steve. I have it here; I think you need to see it.'

Hazel opened her handbag, pulled out a buff envelope and handed it to Matt. He slipped the letter out and studied it. The room fell into silence, broken only by the sound of Hazel munching on a chocolate digestive. It seemed to break Matt's concentration momentarily and he paused to look up. Kate noticed that his gaze was drawn to Hazel's lips as she licked crumbs away from her mouth. *He really fancies her*, thought Kate, *and she is not even trying to come onto him. She looks like she's just come off a catwalk and I have the beginnings of wrinkles around my eyes.*

After a few more seconds, Matt appeared to compose himself again and read on. When he finished, he put the letter down on his knee, shook his head and sighed deeply.

'Did you know about this?' he asked Hazel, fixing her in the eye.

Her face reddened. 'Believe me, I had no idea.'

'Your husband must be in serious trouble to borrow five grand, especially from this lot. Came across them in my previous life. Loan sharks, who take advantage of desperate people.'

'I wish he'd said something; I could have asked Mum

and Dad to help us out. Do you think that Geordie guy on the phone works for them?'

'Leave it with us,' said Matt in a sympathetic tone. 'We will talk to these people and find out what we can. I'll hold onto this letter for now. There is something else I must tell you before we move on, though. We've found out that Steve asked Harry Barton to lend him money on the day he was last seen.'

Hazel's mouth gaped. 'Harry? Really? How much did he ask for?'

'According to Harry, £1000,' said Matt.

'I don't believe this – why the hell didn't he tell me?' cried Hazel, puffing out a forceful breath.

'Perhaps he didn't want to worry you,' said Matt, with little conviction.

Kate sensed it was time to move things on. 'I know this has come as a shock to you, but we'll help you deal with it. Perhaps we can move on to what you came for?'

Hazel nodded her approval and readied herself, sitting bolt upright in the chair. Kate pressed the play button on the tape recorder and they all listened in silence to the rhythmic inflection of the Welsh voice. Hazel was running her fingers around the rim of her coffee mug as she took it in. Kate pushed "stop" and everything went quiet again for a moment before Matt turned to Hazel.

'Do you recognise this person's voice?'

Hazel took a gulp of coffee, then seemed to choke. 'Yuck… swallowed the dregs.' She continued in a croaky voice, 'No… I don't have a cl… clue who this is.'

'We were wondering about this lady,' said Kate. 'She does seem to know your husband well.'

Hazel pursed her lips. 'Her voice isn't familiar.'

'Could she be a friend from your rowing club?' asked Matt. 'Harry Barton mentioned you are members at the Water's Edge.'

'I suppose it's possible. Poor Harry...' She blinked back some tears. 'We used to see a lot of him and Linda. Had a few wild nights in the clubhouse. I don't get down there much now; it's not the same since the accident.'

Matt mirrored her sorrowful face. 'Harry told me about that. Your husband was a lucky man by all accounts.'

Hazel's eyes narrowed. 'What happened to his friends shook him badly. I try to tell him he shouldn't feel guilty, but I know he still does. He's never talked to me about the night of the crash. Says there's no point; it wouldn't help, and I wouldn't understand.'

'Does Steve still go to the club?' asked Kate.

'Yes, he does. Rowing's his passion. Sometimes I think it's even more than that.'

'We'll need to make a few enquiries there. Who's the manager?' asked Matt, his pen poised over his notepad.

'His name's Eddie Fletcher,' replied Hazel, 'but most people call him Fletch.'

# NINE

With no time to lose, Matt had decided it was best to divide and rule. While he was driving west of the city to Beeston, whistling along to "The Model" by Kraftwerk, Kate was on her way to the rowing club. For the next few hours, the office would be manned by his furry ginger friend and an answering device. His route out of the city took him past his old workplace. It was an austere three-storey office block built in grey stone, which had darkened a shade over the years in the city grime. He wondered who occupied his dingey but cosy office in CID these days. *If only I hadn't tried to play the bloody hero. Could be solving serious crimes instead of tracking down adulterers.* Kraftwerk's Moog synthesiser bassline was getting into his head. He remembered to recite his mantra; the police psychologist had called it an affirmation. *I have let go of the past; I have let go of the past… the past is gone; the present's a gift… accept the gift.*

Forcing himself back to the present, he crawled in thick traffic passing the Raleigh cycle factory on his left. The traffic eased as he exited the ring road and drove along University Boulevard. The campus lay on his right with the bust of its famous benefactor, Jesse Boot, set on a white column at the front gates. With his bushy moustache and weather-worn face, Jesse looked more like a wild west hero than an eminent pharmacist. Matt found it strange to think that he now employed one of the university's philosophy graduates. Kate had been too modest to mention it at the interview, but he later found out that she had been awarded a first-class honours degree. *She's a good one, and I'm lucky to have her*, he thought.

Pointing his blue Beetle in the direction of Beeston, he skirted its town centre and turned left, crossing the railway bridge. He followed the direction of Beeston Marina, past a school, before reaching his destination on Meadow Road. He parked his car in front of a dilapidated terraced house, with peeling cream paint on its bay window frames. He noted the absence of a "For Sale" signboard. As yet, there was no sign of Steve's secretary, Monica Purvis, who'd agreed to meet him there. It gave him time to have a nose around outside.

Matt let himself in through a wooden gate, which had been left swinging on one hinge. The house name, "RIVER HAVEN", was on a tarnished brass plaque fixed to the gate. As he clicked it shut, he saw from the corner of his eye the flick of a net curtain in the window of the house next door. He had been spotted.

Matt's cursory inspection of the overgrown front garden turned up a Mars Bar wrapper and an empty packet of Embassy cigarettes. He was about to try the side gate when he heard the sound of a car pulling up outside. He turned around to see Monica Purvis getting out of a Ford Fiesta. She hurried towards him, huffing and puffing as she spoke.

'Sorry to keep you waiting; we got in a flap trying to find the other keys to this place.'

'By the way, did Mr Henson get back in touch?' he asked.

'No. Still angry with us, I suppose,' she said.

Matt pointed to the front garden. 'I see there's no For Sale board.'

'No. Apparently the owners don't want one.'

'Has anyone else viewed it since Steve went missing?'

'No.' She held her breath for a moment. 'And in all the panic, I didn't think to come over here to check it over. You don't think...' Her voice trailed off.

'What?' he asked.

'No, it's a silly idea, forget it. I'll show you inside.'

Monica took a set of keys out of her smart patent leather handbag and opened the front door. She didn't know it, but he was extremely glad of her company. The last time he'd entered an unfamiliar house alone, he'd ended up with a gaping chest. Now he breathed in sickly, musty air as they stepped over the threshold. Monica led him through a cramped and dark hallway to a small living room at the front of the house. A single easy chair sat on a dusty, dog-eared rug, and the wallpaper was smoke stained, with lighter patches where pictures had once hung. Only one picture remained: a striking watercolour which hung lopsided over the fireplace. It depicted water rushing over a stepped weir into a wide, tree-lined river. The tall trees were bending in the wind, and there were dark rain clouds in the sky.

'How long has this place been empty?' he asked.

'About six months now. The owners have moved abroad. What with the recession and—'

She was interrupted by the creaking of floorboards above her head. They looked at one another for a few moments in stunned silence. Matt put his forefinger to his lips. As he did so, the squeaking noise started up again. It was unmistakably the sound of someone's footsteps. He moved stealthily back to the hallway and called up the stairs.

'Hello. We are from the estate agents. Maybe you want to come down and tell us what you're doing here?'

Monica, who was now close by Matt's side, called out in anguish. 'Steve. Is that you?'

They both stood for a few seconds, eyes fixed on the landing for any sign of movement. Then there was a click followed shortly by a loud thud which seemed to come from the back of the house. Matt signalled for Monica to stay where she was while he sped up the stairs. He pushed open the first door he came to and stood aside, but there was nobody to be seen inside the small bedroom which overlooked the street. Heart racing, he crept along the dark landing towards the next room. The door was open and, peering into it, he saw a wide-open window. When he got to the window, he saw that it opened onto a flat-roofed extension to the back of the house. He heard a gate opening and then the loud patter of running feet. He fast footed it downstairs, then ran straight out through the front door past an open-mouthed Monica.

When he got to the pavement, he first looked left, towards the canal, but saw nothing. Turning the other way, he saw a man about fifty yards away running at pace past the school gate, in the direction of the town. Matt shouted as he gave chase. 'Stop! Come back here!' He ran another thirty yards, but then lost sight of the intruder behind parked cars on a bend in the road. Matt slowed, scanning the street in all directions, but when he reached the next junction a few seconds later, the guy had vanished. He was panting heavily and had to rest his hands on his knees for half a minute, before trudging slowly back to the house.

Monica was waiting for him at the front gate, her face etched with concern.

'Did you see who it was?' she asked.

'Not really,' said Matt, still annoyed he'd been given the slip. 'Only got the back view. Enough to make out he had dark hair and was wearing jeans and a denim jacket. Why did you think it might be Steve?'

Blood rushed to her cheeks. 'I don't know really. I suppose he hasn't been himself these past few weeks. This might seem crazy, but I thought he might have used this place to hide out.'

Matt fixed her in the eye. 'I think it's time you levelled with me. Is your boss in some kind of trouble?'

She sighed heavily. 'Steve's a good talker, but he's not very good with money. His accountant is always telling him to be more cautious.'

'Who's that?'

'Mr Travers.'

*My ex-wife's boyfriend, no less. Knowing Guy Travers,*

*the only thing he'll be worried about is getting his extortionate fees paid*, thought Matt.

'Just how serious are his money problems?'

Monica cleared her throat. 'I don't know for sure. We've had a few unexpected callers at the office in the past week.'

'Who were they?'

'One was a restaurant owner. He said Steve paid him with a cheque that bounced; he was not best pleased.'

'Which restaurant was it?'

'The Rhinegold.'

'And the other visitor?'

'Our signboard maker, Mr Carter. He told me he hadn't been paid for six months and was fed up of being fobbed off.'

'Is there anything else you can tell me?'

She strummed her bottom lip with her forefinger. 'There was a well-dressed man who was reluctant to say why he wanted Steve.'

'Did you find out?'

'No, but he seemed very annoyed that Steve was not there. On his way out he threw his calling card on my desk; his name's Ken Marchant and he's in the construction business.'

'I'll need to see that card. Have you still got it?'

'Yes, it's in a drawer with the others.' Monica frowned as she glanced back towards the front door. 'It's a real mess in there. I'll have to get the whole place cleaned up and disinfected.'

'I'll inform the police about the intruder. It might help if someone kept an eye on the house for a while.'

'I'm sorry, I should have checked sooner.'

Matt could see the distress in her eyes. 'I don't think *you* are to blame here.'

Monica blushed, then slid back the sleeve of her jacket to look at her watch. 'I'm sorry but I must go now. I'm needed back at the office.'

'Mind if I stay on a little longer?' asked Matt.

'Not at all,' said Monica, 'you can drop the keys off later.'

# TEN

Kate was not in the best frame of mind as she drew up in her Mini at the embankment, overlooked by the towering stands at the Forest ground. Luke had called her at the office just as she was leaving. *For someone who begged me to stay and work things out, he seems in a big hurry to get this divorce through*, she thought. *Wonder if he's still seeing the Barbie Doll from the tennis club?* She was disappointed in Luke, but even more so in herself. That she had been so easily taken in. That she had actually thought the love she felt for him was returned. She adjusted the rear-view mirror to check her make-up and ran a brush through her hair.

Stepping out of the car, Kate took in some much-needed fresh air. A stiff breeze was in her face as she crossed the road to the Water's Edge boat club. It was a bright white building, and her eyes were taken by a large insignia painted on it over the first-floor balcony. The royal blue club badge in the shape of a shield bore the motto "*Per Ardua ad Meta*" and a pair of crossed oars. Latin was not her strong point. Matt, she had no doubt, would have instantly translated it had he been there.

She approached the front of the clubhouse and peered into the boat room. Its double doors were wide open, and in the dim light, she could make out a stocky man in a tracksuit walking in her direction through a muddle of racing boats and oars. Some of the boats were stored upside down on steel racks, others were upright on trestles, or even strewn across the floor.

He had the ruddy complexion of someone who spent time outdoors and smiled when he made eye contact. 'Mrs Brooks? I'm Eddie. I'm the chief dogsbody around here.'

She gestured over his shoulder towards the boat storage room. 'Looks like you've got a job on your hands.'

'You're telling me. But from what you said on the phone, so have you. What's my old mate Steve been up to then?'

'I was hoping you could help me find out. Is there somewhere we could…?'

'Follow me. Haven't got long, mind.'

Eddie led the way up a wooden staircase on the outside of the building which led to the balcony. To their left, the river flowed through the triple arches of Trent Bridge. He unlocked a door which took them into a low-ceilinged bar area. The air inside carried the smell of stale beer. He ushered Kate to a table with two chairs, then continued to the back of the room to switch the lights on. She took her notebook from her handbag and by the time he came back, her pen was poised over it.

'As you know, we have been hired by Hazel Mackie to find her missing husband.'

He rubbed his chin. 'Your call came as a bit of a shock. How long has Steve been AWOL?'

'He's been gone a whole week now, I'm afraid. When was it you last saw him?'

Eddie paused a moment. 'That'd be about three weeks ago, I reckon.'

'Can you give me an exact date?'

'He's normally here Friday afternoons.'

Kate clicked open her briefcase and pulled out her Filofax. She ran her finger down the calendar at the front. 'Then, that would be Friday, 11 March, is that right?'

Eddie shrugged his shoulders. 'Guess so.'

Kate made a hasty note in her book. 'Did he go rowing that day?'

'Not as I recall.'

'See anyone with him?'

'Yeah, one of our lady rowers, Linda Barton.'

'Harry Barton's wife.'

'That's her. Harry was one of our top oarsmen before his accident.'

'Yes, I heard about that. Such a terrible thing to happen.'

Eddie scrubbed a hand over his face. 'Met Linda, have you?'

'No, but my boss has. Must be difficult for her, with a young daughter too.'

'Yep, that's true. Think that's why she likes coming down here, to escape it all for a bit.'

'And meet up with old friends?' she asked with a tilt

of the head. 'How did Steve seem to you that last time you saw him?'

'He'd had a few too many, but he looked right enough to me when he left.'

'And Linda?'

'Yeah, they were having a few laughs.'

'Would you say they were enjoying one another's company?'

Eddie affected a puzzled look. 'I don't know what you mean.'

She looked him squarely in the eye. 'Don't give me that, Mr Fletcher. What I mean is, did they leave together?'

He shifted in his chair, shuffling his feet. 'That evening? Can't say for sure, but she gives him a lift sometimes.'

Kate paused. 'They meet here quite often then?'

'Every couple of weeks, I'd say.'

'They row together?'

'No. They prefer to single scull.'

'What about Hazel Mackie? Do you see much of her?'

'Not these days, no. She comes down with Steve now and then, but it must be over a year since I've seen her on the water.'

'Does Steve have any other good friends here? Hazel told us a guy with a Geordie accent called Steve recently. Does that ring a bell?'

He gave her a puzzled look. 'Not anyone I recognise from here, I'm afraid.' He checked his watch. 'Well, if that's all, I'll have to be—'

She held up the palm of her hand. 'Just one more thing, Mr Fletcher. I've been wondering, what does your club motto mean?'

He smiled. 'Ah… noticed that, did you? *Per Ardua ad Meta*. It means through adversity to the goal.'

She chuckled. 'Sounds more like football than rowing to me.'

# ELEVEN

Matt took the keys from Monica and watched her walk back to her car before turning back to the house. As he made his way towards the front door, he heard a loud thud behind him. He stopped in his tracks; dark and bloody flashbacks raced through his head. His heart was racing and the more he told himself not to panic, the quicker it seemed to beat. He spun quickly around and saw the front gate crash into the post in the freshening wind. Cursing himself for being so jumpy, he sat down outside the house, his back against the front wall. He closed his eyes. *Breathe slowly; think of your special place... You are sitting in a garden... The sun is beating on your face... Trees are casting shadows over the lawn... The only sound is birdsong... You feel relaxed; there is nothing to disturb you. You are safe.* He stayed there for a few minutes until his head had cleared and he no longer feared he was going to die. Then he got to his feet, walked slowly over the threshold and began a closer inspection of the premises.

There were the remains of a fish and chip supper in greasy paper on the kitchen table next to a bottle of curdled milk, giving off a rancid odour. Upstairs, he found a sleeping bag on the floor of the main bedroom and a pair of thick woollen socks, worn through at the heels. He found cobwebs in the bath and thick black mould growing on the wall behind the toilet. He checked the front and back doors and all the windows but couldn't find any signs of a break-in. Deciding to look outside, he found an empty whisky bottle near the back door and cigarette ends scattered on the crazy paving. There was a rusting fork embedded in a flower bed, a green plastic watering can and a length of thick rope, which he found behind the compost heap near the back fence. As he turned on his heels to head back towards the house, an elderly lady with curlers in her hair was pegging out her washing next door. He guessed that it had been her behind the net curtains earlier.

'You looking at the house?' she asked, eyeing him up and down with suspicion.

'Not really. Actually, I'm looking for someone. I've got his picture if you wouldn't mind taking—'

'And who might you be, mister?'

'Matt Crawford, private detective.'

'A snoop you say… what are you doing here, then?'

'The man I'm looking for came here just before he went missing.'

The old lady narrowed her eyes. 'How do I know you're who you say you are?'

Matt pulled out his wallet and took out his business card and the Polaroid of Steve. 'I have proof of who I am and a photo of the person I'm looking for. Would you mind taking a look?'

She scratched her head, then bent down to put her clothes pegs on the floor. 'Alright then, hand them over.'

Matt passed them to her over the garden fence. She squinted as she gave the photo and Matt's calling card a closer inspection. She sighed and passed them back to him. 'Yes, I have seen him here a couple of times. Who is he?'

'He's the estate agent selling this house. Do you remember when you last saw him?'

'It's a good while back, more than a month I'd say. He was showing a young couple around the garden, such as it is. The place is going to rack and ruin. Now, if you don't mind, I'll have to be getting on.' She picked up a damp pillowcase from her wicker basket and pegged it to the line.

Matt was looking ruefully at the photo of Steve. 'If it's okay, I've got a couple more things to ask you.'

She glanced down at her pile of wet clothes. 'Well, make it quick. This washing won't dry itself.'

'Have you seen anyone here in the last seven days?'

She scratched her chin and paused for a moment. 'Well… I did notice someone in the back yesterday afternoon. Thought he was a gardener or something.'

'What did he look like?'

'Didn't see his face; he was having a fag near the back fence. Tall with dark hair. He was wearing jeans and a checked lumberjack shirt.'

'And what about last Wednesday afternoon? Do you remember if you saw or heard anything then?'

She crinkled her nose. 'Wednesday's my shopping day. Yes, now I think of it, when I came back there was a blue van parked outside. I noticed it because one of the back lights was smashed.'

'What make was it?'

She squinted. 'Search me. It was a big one, a sort of transit van.'

'What time was this?'

'School kids were coming out. About 3.30pm, I guess.'

'Did you see anyone here?'

'No, not a soul. But that's not unusual. Lots of them park here to go walking along the canal.'

'How long did it stay?'

'Quite a while. But it had gone by morning.' Her face dropped a little. 'Don't suppose I've been much help to you, have I?'

'I wouldn't say that, Mrs…?'

'Tindall.'

'Thank you for your help, Mrs Tindall, there is just one more thing.'

'Yes?'

'The guy you thought was a gardener. It's possible he's been sleeping rough here. I am going to inform the police, so don't be surprised if they turn up some time soon. We disturbed him earlier, so I doubt you'll see him again.'

\*\*\*

Matt locked up the house and walked back onto the street, still processing what Mrs Tindall had just told him. He paused by the gate to scribble in his notebook. Then he pocketed it and turned to his left in the direction of the canal. In the distance he could see the tops of moored boats bobbing up and down in the breeze. In just two minutes he reached the towpath. His eyes were drawn to the ripples on the water, and he felt that unique calmness he only experienced when he was near the sea, a lake or a river. He was glad to be outside again.

Looking to his right he could see a small iron bridge in the distance and headed in that direction. As he got closer, he could see that there was a lock gate just beyond the bridge. A bearded boatman was bent over the winding mechanism which opened the lock, sweat trickling down his cheek. Then, as Matt continued his walk, the smell of cooking wafted across his path. It reminded him of Saturday mornings growing up, his dad standing over the cooker with a frying pan full of sizzling bacon and spluttering eggs. His fried bread was legendary. He missed the old boy: their pub conversations about politics, watching football on the telly and his dry humour. His dad said little about his job as a police sergeant and never spoke about wartime in the force. Matt's mum told him that his dad had been "very brave". That was enough to make him a hero in Matt's eyes.

After a few more steps, which took him past a chandlery, the source of the tempting aroma came into view. The Marina Café looked like one you would come across in a seaside town. A white frontage, with the menu painted on big picture windows. A windswept couple sat outside at a table, the steam rising from their drinks mingling with cigarette smoke. Passing them by, he entered the café and walked up to the counter. He waited his turn before ordering a coffee and bacon cob from a cheerful, rosy-cheeked lady in a pin-striped apron. He took a seat at a window table and looked out over the marina, where some of the larger river cruisers were moored. *For all I know, Steve could be hiding himself in one of these*, he thought.

To his disappointment, the bacon was undercooked, and the coffee was insipid. He took his plate and mug back to the counter and handed them to his smiling host.

'You can stay if you like, clear the rest of the tables,' she said.

'I think I'll pass on that, but there is something you can do for *me*.'

'What's that?' she asked, pushing a strand of blonde hair behind her ear.

Matt pulled the photo of Steve Mackie from his pocket and held it up in front of her. 'Ever seen this guy around here?'

'Not that I remember, and I think I would. Good looker, isn't he? Reminds me of that actor, what's his name?'

'Kirk Douglas?'

'Yeah, that's the one. What's he done?'

'Disappeared a week ago. The last person to see him was a taxi driver who dropped him off on Meadow Road last Wednesday.'

'Are you police?'

'No. I'm an investigator working for the missing man's wife.'

She frowned. 'Bet she's in a state, poor woman.'

'Yes, she's desperate for news. Maybe you could help me with one last thing. Have you seen a blue transit van around here recently? With a smashed rear light?'

'No, can't say as I have. But you could ask up at the recreation ground. Lots of folk park there and walk their dogs.'

'Where's that?'

'Go back to the lock and walk over the canal bridge. You can't miss it. Once you cross over the bridge, you'll be looking straight at it. It's up by the weir.'

Matt left the café and started to walk back along the towpath, deep in thought. He passed a couple of hikers on a bench, taking a drink from a flask. Above them, a pair of herring gulls was gliding on the air streams, ready to swoop down into the river to feed. Soon afterwards the lock came into view. *You can't miss it, she'd said. Maybe that was the point. Was there something staring him right in the face about Steve Mackie that he'd missed?*

# TWELVE

Desmond came running out from Matt's room when Kate came through the main office door. The cat purred loudly as she stroked his back, then when he'd had enough of the fuss, he turned away and started to walk in the direction of the kitchen. Following him, she poured dry nibbles into an empty stainless steel bowl placed in the centre of a mat on the floor. While the ravenous cat was crunching his way through these, she made herself a coffee and walked back to her desk.

Kate opened a drawer and pulled out a Tupperware container. She removed the lid and took out a large wedge of chocolate cake. Biting into it, the taste of rich, gooey chocolate seemed to soothe her soul. A couple more mouthfuls later, her appetite was sated. She wiped her hands with a tissue, then opened the file on her desk. The telephone number she was looking for was on the top sheet. She picked up the handset and hit the keys of the dial. After six rings, her call was answered by a gruff male voice.

'Hello, who's that?'

'This is Kate Brooks. Is that Mr Henson?'

There was a grunt. 'No.'

'Is he there? Can he come to the phone?' she asked.

'Nobody here by that name; this is a telephone box. I was just getting the coins out of my pocket when you rang.'

'Oh, I'm sorry, I must have been given the wrong number. Can I just check it with you?'

He read the number on the call box phone back to her and it was exactly the same as the one she had written down.

'The number I have appears to be correct,' she said.

'Maybe you just dialled it wrong,' he said. 'Anyway I must—'

'Just before you go. Can you tell me where you are?'

He started to cough and had trouble stopping. Kate recognised the retching sound; her dad was a heavy smoker. Still spluttering, the man finally got out his words. 'Anson Avenue… Beeston… near the post office.'

Kate thanked him and put the phone down. *Not surprising I got no answer when I tried before*, she thought. Mr Henson's address had been written underneath his phone number: *13, Barlow Drive, Beeston*. She pulled the Nottingham A–Z Atlas from her drawer and opened it to check the location. 'Bingo! It's just off Anson Avenue,' she muttered to herself. Kate's first instinct was to drive straight there, but she guessed that Matt wouldn't want her to leave station right now. She strummed her fingers on the desk. *Hope he'll be back soon.* After she'd swept up the crumbs of the cake, she took a sip from her coffee mug. It was the one that Matt had given her for her thirty-second birthday, just last year. The mug was white and had black lettering which was set out like a dictionary entry:

"KATE. Noun. 1. A very sweet girl. 2. Likes to eat chocolate cake. 3. Drives me nuts".

*What would it say if this were Steve Mackie's mug?* thought Kate. *Maybe something like "Enjoys the high life. Runs up bills he can't pay. Likes the company of beautiful women".*

Kate thought about how Hazel would be feeling right now. First her husband goes missing, then people she doesn't know are trying to track him down and the press are hounding her. Kate had noticed Hazel's tetchiness when they had played her the answerphone message earlier. She wondered if Hazel knew about Steve's womanising. Maybe she was turning a blind eye and telling herself it would all blow over in time? Kate had fallen into the same trap with Luke. And that hadn't exactly ended well.

# THIRTEEN

Matt walked briskly over the canal bridge in the direction of a large brick-built sports pavilion which overlooked the playing fields. When he reached it, he opened the heavy metal front door and found himself in a gloomy foyer. To his right was a green door marked "CARETAKER'S OFFICE". He knocked before letting himself in. Inside, a bespectacled, stocky man in his forties sat at a desk behind the counter reading the *Daily Mirror* while biting on a finger of Kit-Kat. As Matt approached, the caretaker paused, swallowed his last bite of chocolate biscuit and peered over at him.

'You come about the fence?' he asked, getting slowly to his feet and shuffling in Matt's direction.

'Afraid not,' said Matt, 'sorry to disappoint you.'

The big man gave a deep sigh. 'Been waiting all day for the council to turn up to see to the damage down by the river. Had a bit of trouble here recently. Teenage vandals and joy riders. So, what can I do for you then? Want to make a booking?'

'No, but I could do with some help if you've got a few moments.'

'Help with what?' asked the caretaker.

'There's a man gone missing, last seen not far from here. I'm trying to find him.'

'Gone missing, near the river you say? You'll be lucky. Who are you exactly?'

'I'm a private investigator working for his wife.'

The caretaker looked Matt up and down, scrutinising his features. 'You don't look much like one to me.'

Matt chuckled. 'Been watching *Public Eye* on the telly, I suppose? We don't all wear gaberdine macs and look like Alfred Burke, you know.' He slipped his business card from his inside pocket and placed it on the counter. 'My credentials are on there.'

The caretaker picked up the card and nodded in Matt's direction. 'Okay, who is it you're looking for?'

'His name's Steve Mackie. I've got his photo here,' said Matt, handing the man the Polaroid holiday snap of the missing man.

The caretaker took a close look, then shook his head. 'Sorry, Mr Crawford, can't help you. Never seen this bloke before.'

Matt rubbed the back of his neck. 'That's a blow, I was hoping you might have. There is something else, though. Have you seen a blue transit van parked up here in the past week or so? You might have noticed a cracked rear light?'

The man scratched his head. 'No, can't help you there either.'

The detective gave a sigh. 'Well, if you do see a blue van or the man in the photo, give me a call. The number's on my card. Believe you me, I'll make it worth your while.'

His curiosity aroused by what the caretaker had said about vandals, Matt made his way back though the gloomy pavilion and back out into the light. Taking a path to the right, and with his hands in his jacket pockets, he walked in the direction of the river. As he ascended a steep bank, he could hear a loud gushing noise. He stopped at the top to gather his breath before scanning the scene from on high. It looked somehow familiar. Then it dawned on him: the watercolour in the living room at River Haven. It had been painted from another perspective, but it was undoubtedly the same scene, the water rushing over the concrete steps of the weir and the tree-lined riverbank beyond.

Looking to his left, he saw a road leading down to the river. It was skirted by a tall chain-link fence. He walked down the embankment and onto the road. Heading down to the river, the road curved sharply left. On the apex of the bend, he saw a huge tear in the fence; one of the posts had been pushed back at an angle. Matt stepped onto the verge to take a closer look. There were deep tyre marks in the grass, which ran out just the other side of the fence. The vehicle must have been travelling at speed to rip through it. Matt knelt down to examine the ground. There were several flakes of blue paint scattered among the blades of grass. The size of the tyre prints and the colour of the paint suggested they could belong to the van the neighbour had told him about. Satisfied he'd seen enough, Matt started to walk back up the road towards the canal bridge. As he did so, he heard a squawking sound coming from the direction of the river.

Following his ears, he turned back and descended the road which led to the water's edge. Walking across a pebbled path, he saw two coots with prominent white foreheads squabbling near a wide expanse of reed bed. A sudden gust of wind rustled the reeds, and as they swayed, he saw something nestling amongst them. From a distance it looked like a very rare and colourful plant. He took ten steps along the bank to get a better look. It was only when he got up close that he could make out what it was. It had become entangled in the long blades. When he saw it, he let out a gasp. It was a floral tie.

# FOURTEEN

There was a look of surprise on the caretaker's face when Matt burst back into his office.

'I need to use your phone,' said Matt, in a commanding voice.

The man stood up and crossed his arms over his chest. 'I'm afraid I can't just—'

Matt's jaw stiffened. 'Look, this is really urgent.'

The caretaker relented. He opened the flap in the counter and let Matt through. He gestured for Matt to use his chair to make the call. The detective punched in the numbers and was glad to hear Kate's dulcet tones on the line.

'Crawford Detective Agency, how can I help?'

'Kate, it's me. I'm over at Beeston weir and I think we might have made a breakthrough. Can you give Hazel Mackie a call? Say we are just checking a few more details.

Ask if she can remember what Steve was wearing on the day he disappeared. I need as much detail as possible.'

'Has Steve been spotted?'

'I'll tell you everything later. Just make the call, would you? Ring me back as soon as you've spoken to her.'

He gave her his number and put the receiver down. The caretaker was hovering nearby, but Matt stayed put in his chair.

'I need to wait for a call.'

The caretaker's eyes widened. 'Think you're onto something, do you?'

'Don't know for sure. Tell me, when did you find out the fence was broken?'

'Been down there, have you? I noticed it a few days ago when the groundsman was giving the field a mow.'

'When exactly?'

He stroked his chin. 'Let me think… I needed it done for the football on Saturday. Must have been last Friday. A bloody mess, isn't it? If you ask me, whoever was driving never passed a test. Probably too young to even take one.'

'Did you call the police?' asked Matt.

The caretaker shrugged his shoulders. 'No point. Never saw nothing.'

'But you think you know who might have done it?'

'Got a darned good idea. There's four lads always hanging around the car park.'

'How old?'

'Fourteen, maybe fifteen. School kids. Not that they turn up there very often.'

'Got any names for me?' asked Matt.

'No, but I can tell you what they look—'

The trill of the phone interrupted him. He reached over the desk and picked up the receiver.

'Kate who? I see… yes, he's here.' The caretaker handed the phone to Matt.

'Hazel's just called back,' she said, catching her breath. 'She says Steve was wearing a grey, pin-striped suit, a white shirt and his favourite tie.'

'Stop there. What sort of tie?'

'She said it's big and flowery. Pink and green.'

'Thank you, that's exactly what I needed to know. I owe you.'

'Just doing my job; anyway, are you going to tell me what's happened now?'

'I'll fill you in when I get back. Can you hold the fort for a while longer?'

She chuckled. 'Look after Desmond, you mean. Sure.'

Matt put his finger on the switch to end the call and held it down, keeping the handset close to his ear. Without a word to the caretaker, he dialled again. He had the number in his head. A familiar voice answered the phone; it was a switchboard operator at Police Central. He asked to be put through to DI Joe Martin.

# FIFTEEN

Daylight was beginning to fade. The street lights were coming on, like a second dawn illuminating the city's buildings. The elegant ancient churches, courthouse and council offices as well as the modern high-rise flats. Workers were spilling out of the factories, offices and shops. Pubs and restaurants were bracing themselves for the influx of customers. Kate was beginning to wonder what could have kept Matt so long and, in their office kitchen, Desmond was miaowing loudly while pacing around his empty food bowl. Kate put the last of the files she had taken from her desk into the cabinet and locked it. As she was walking to the kitchen, the phone rang. She turned on her heels and hurried to pick it up.

'Matt, is that you?'

'Sorry to disappoint you. It's Keith.'

'Hi, Keith, what can I do for you?'

'Did you like my piece on your missing person?'

'Yes, I did; your headline grabbed my attention. "FEARS GROW FOR MISSING ESTATE AGENT". It's good.'

'Thanks, I thought so too.'

'Might prick someone's conscience and make them come forward,' she said.

'Hope so. The boss has asked me to do a follow-up, you know, from the human angle. What his family and friends are going through and so on.'

'I look forward to seeing it,' she said, with little enthusiasm in her voice. She knew his main motive was to sell papers. He wouldn't fret if the search went on a good while longer.

There was a pause at the other end of the line. 'But there is one major problem. Mrs Mackie is not answering my calls. I was just wondering if you might put in a good word for an old workmate?'

'I don't think I can help you there. Mrs Mackie has made it very clear to us that she doesn't want to speak to the press. That goes for all of you, I'm afraid. So, if that's all, Keith, I must be getting—'

He cleared his throat. 'Actually, there is one more thing. I'd like to thank you for letting me break the story. Could I take you to dinner one night?'

'I really don't—'

His voice softened. 'For old time's sake. It's just a meal.'

'Really? Now there I was thinking you might want to ask me about the Mackies.'

'What if I promise not to mention their name the whole evening?'

'Alright. I'll think about it.'

As she put the phone down, the cat emerged from the kitchen with a face as long as a fiddle. She walked up to him and stroked his back. He did an about-turn and led her back in the direction of food. As Kate was spooning the last of the tin into his bowl, she heard the office door opening.

'Anyone at home?' called Matt.

'We're here, in the kitchen. It's feeding time.'

He put his head around the door, smiling at them both. 'Got anything left? I'm starving.'

'Only if you like Whiskas with tuna.'

'I'll pass on that one, but if there's any coffee going?'

Five minutes later, Kate brought two coffees and a plate of chocolate digestives through to Matt's office for their debrief. He was barely taking a pause to breathe as he told the story of his visit to River Haven and his fruitless chase after the mysterious intruder. When he told her about discovering the tie by the riverbank, her mouth fell open.

'You really think it's Steve's?'

'Yes. I recognised it from a picture hanging on his office wall. So, as soon as Hazel confirmed that he was wearing it that day, I alerted the police.'

'How did they respond?'

'DI Martin and his team showed up in minutes and they've sent police dogs along the riverbank and a team of divers into the water.'

'Did they find anything?'

'Yes. Some rocks they found down by the river were stained with what looks like blood.'

'And are they still searching?'

'When the light faded, they called the divers in. I think they're still combing the woods near the river by torchlight.'

Kate pursed her lips. 'Have you told Hazel?'

'Yes. She's been with me at the marina all afternoon. I picked her up from home.'

'How is she holding up?'

'She looks like someone lost in a maze. When DI Martin showed her the tie, she went a whiter shade of pale. She seems certain it's Steve's. We both joined the search until darkness fell; I could see she was exhausted, so I persuaded her to let me drop her off at home on my way here.'

Kate dunked a biscuit and took a bite from it before continuing. 'Do you think the man at the house has anything to do with Steve's disappearance?'

'Could be connected, I suppose. We'd know a lot more if I could only run faster.'

She drew a deep breath. 'Mr Crawford, you are in no fit state to go chasing after people. What were you thinking?'

He rubbed his palm on his shirt in the area of the chest wound. 'Sometimes I forget. By the way, you've got chocolate on your chin.'

She wiped the smudge away with her finger. 'What if he'd turned on you? Did you think about that?'

'Not really.'

She frowned. 'Did you at least get a good look at him?'

'Only saw his back, and he was too far away. The neighbour saw him too, over the garden fence. But she didn't see his face either.'

'Not much to go on then?'

'Well, we know he'd been sleeping there. But I couldn't find any sign of a forced entry.'

'That's strange. Maybe someone left a window open,' she offered.

'Well, it's a possibility, I suppose,' said Matt. 'By the way, how did it go at the boat club?'

'It seems our missing man has been meeting up there with Linda Barton.'

'Gets around a bit our Mr Mackie.'

'The word is she gives him a lift home,' said Kate.

'That's all?' asked Matt, then bit into a digestive.

'That's all the manager would say.'

He sighed. 'Steve's screwing his friend's wife. Wonder what else Linda hasn't told us? Better have another word with her, alone.'

'You'll find her at the rowing club most Fridays according to Eddie Fletcher. But I've got more news for you. The number you gave me for the viewer, Henson, turns out it's a telephone box.'

Matt raised his eyebrows. 'How did you find out?'

'When I rang it, someone picked up. He gave me the location too.'

'Where is it?'

'It's in Beeston, near a post office. I checked on the street map and Henson lives close by.'

'Good work, lass. Let's drop in on Mr Henson in the morning, on our way to the marina.'

# DAY FOUR

Thursday, 31 March 1983

# SIXTEEN

It was 8am, and they were in Matt's car. Kate had the Nottingham A–Z on her lap and was tracing their route along the page with her index finger. 'Turn left here and then take the next right. That should be Barlow Avenue.'

The avenue was quiet in the early morning gloom. The houses all looked the same. Solidly built post-war semis with white pebble-dash rendering and a single bay window to the front. Matt slowed his Beetle to a snail's pace as they looked for Mr Henson's house.

'There's number eleven, so it should be that next one on the left,' said Kate, pointing to a house with an overgrown privet hedge in the front garden. She looked puzzled for a moment as Matt pulled up outside.

'Wait a minute – this isn't right; the sign says fifteen. We must have gone too far.'

'We'll park here anyway,' said Matt, climbing out of the car.

They walked back in the direction they'd come, only to find that this was number eleven.

Matt scratched his head as they stood facing one another on the pavement in bemusement. 'Number thirteen has disappeared it seems. Let's give this one a try anyway.'

Matt opened the gate and ushered Kate through. They walked down a short path side by side before Matt stepped up to the porch and gave the brass knocker on the front door a couple of raps. A dog started to bark and then they heard someone shouting for the door to be answered. After another twenty seconds, the door opened slowly and a young woman in jeans and a jumper stood in front of them in the doorway. She had long, straggly dark hair, with a low fringe nearly hiding her eyes. She crossed her arms as she spoke. 'Come about the rent, have you?'

'Actually, no we haven't,' said Kate. 'We are from the estate agents. We are looking for Mr Henson at number thirteen.'

The woman gave a throaty laugh. 'Well, good luck with that. Never heard of no Mr Henson and there ain't a number thirteen in this street.'

Kate looked confused. 'No number thirteen?'

'The council decided to skip it because it's unlucky. They thought people wouldn't want to live there. Load of nonsense if you ask me.'

Kate exchanged knowing looks with Matt before thanking the lady for her trouble and turning back towards the pavement. Back inside the car, they sat in silence for a few seconds before Matt spoke.

'We need to find this Mr Henson, if that is his real name. Let's see if Monica can describe him for us.'

'And then what?' asked Kate.

'I'll see if that brother of mine can find any record of him. Could be he's been in trouble before.'

\*\*\*

Mist was hanging over the canal as Kate and Matt approached the police cordon at the marina. In contrast to yesterday, the air was still and carried a dank smell. They weaved their way through a cluster of press reporters and interested onlookers who had gathered to see what was going on. Kate saw Keith Ferrell in the midst of the throng, but he had not seen her. He was deep in conversation with a man in the crowd. Head down, she followed Matt closely as he cleared a path to the front. The PC on duty recognised Matt, and they were allowed through. Kate saw her boss looking all around him as they walked towards the river. But it was Kate who spotted their client first and pointed her out. Hazel was sitting alone, shoulders hunched, on a wooden bench that looked out over the weir. As they approached, she got to her feet to greet them. She smiled nervously at Matt.

'I'm so glad you came. It's been one heck of a morning with the police asking me all these questions. They're acting as if I had something to do with all of this.' A teardrop rolled down her pale cheek. 'Do they have any idea what I'm going through?'

Matt shook his head. 'I'm sorry we weren't here earlier. As far as the police go, there's really no need to be concerned. They are just following procedure and no more. They are trying to gather as much information as they can to help find Steve.'

Hazel looked wistfully towards the fast-flowing river. 'Do you think he's in there somewhere? DI Martin seems sure of it. He asked me all these questions about Steve's state of mind and if I knew about anything that was troubling him.'

'Again, it's just routine,' said Matt.

Hazel looked across to Kate for reassurance. 'I don't think Steve would do anything like that. He has too much to live for.'

Kate understood why she would say this; it was too hard to even contemplate. But in her own mind, she was working on the same theory as the police. With what they knew about Steve's perilous finances, it would add up. Or maybe he'd left the tie in the reed bed to make them think that. She couldn't voice any of this now. Their client looked totally washed out.

'How long have you been here?' asked Kate.

Pulling up her coat sleeve, Hazel looked at her watch. 'Nearly three hours.'

'Fancy a coffee?' asked Kate. 'There's a café a short walk from here.'

Hazel hesitated. 'I don't know if—'

'We can tell the on-duty PC where we are,' said Matt.

They sat at a corner table inside the Marina Café, steam swirling from their drinks. The only other customers were two dog walkers who had tethered their pets to an outside bench while they chatted over a mug of tea and a cigarette. Matt and Kate were sitting opposite Hazel, who had her back to the window.

Hazel took a sip of hot coffee and fidgeted uncomfortably in her chair.

'I had a call last night,' she said.

Matt tilted his head. 'Tell us more.'

'Steve's accountant. Asking about him.'

'Guy Travers?' asked Matt.

Hazel's eyes widened. 'You know him then?'

'Steve's secretary mentioned him,' said Matt, deciding to skip over Guy's connection to his ex-wife Amanda.

'I told him about the search. It turns out he needs Steve to sign some papers.'

'His tax return?' asked Matt.

'No. It's for a business loan. Steve's agreed a deal on a plot of land in Stapleford and plans to build new apartments on it.'

Matt raised an eyebrow. 'Did you know about this?'

Her nostrils flared. 'No, I didn't. So, after I'd put the phone down, I went searching in the study. Do you know what I found in his desk?'

'What?'

'A letter from the Abbey National addressed to Steve. Without a word to me, he's remortgaged our house. Six months ago.' She threw both hands in the air and paused, anticipating a response. But Matt was staring over her shoulder. He was distracted by the person advancing towards the café from the towpath. He recognised his wispy grey hair and short, scuttling strides. DI Joe Martin slowed as he entered the café. There was a grim twist to his mouth. Hazel now turned to see who it was and called out to him as he neared their table.

'Do you have any news?'

The inspector shuffled to a halt in front of Hazel and narrowed his eyes. 'I'd like you to come with me. Our divers have found someone.'

# SEVENTEEN

It was the middle of the afternoon. Kate was at her typewriter, trying to concentrate on the letter Matt had dictated but with her mind still on the morning's discovery. She heard the office door click open and Matt strode in with a white cardboard box in his arms. He placed it on the desk in front of her.

'It's my way of saying thank you.'

'For what?'

'For working long hours and not complaining, for looking after my cat, for putting up with—'

She held her hand up. 'Stop there, my head is getting bigger by the second.'

Matt smiled. 'Okay then, I'll go and make tea while it returns to its normal size.'

While he made his way to the kitchen, Kate opened up the box. Nestled inside was a generous slice of black forest gateau. Matt returned five minutes later with two mugs of tea, a side plate and a cake fork. Kate had added this essential item to their cutlery tray at the end of her first week with the agency. She sipped her tea before taking a first taste of rich chocolate and sour cherries. 'Thank you – this is delicious. Don't you want to share?'

'No thanks – it's all yours. By the way, any luck with a description of our Mr Henson?'

'Yes, I've made a note of what Monica said.' She reached across the desk for her pad and started to read from it. 'Short cropped dark hair, about six foot tall and broad shouldered. Late twenties or early thirties with a boxer's nose, flat and offset. Some acne scars on his cheeks. Had a local accent.'

'Well done. I'll get the details to my brother. See if he can turn something up for us.'

'Monica was in a state; she'd heard about the police search. Do you think they'll have identified his body yet?' she asked.

'Maybe. Depends on the time it has been in the water. After a few days, the flesh will start to decompose.'

Kate crinkled her nose. 'Hadn't thought of that. Maybe we shouldn't have left Hazel like that.'

'We had no choice. DI Martin made it crystal clear that we were persona non grata.'

'Doesn't seem right though, does it? Without your intervention, they would never have found the body in the first place.'

He shrugged his shoulders. 'That's the way it works.'

Kate flushed with indignation. 'Then, when it's all wound up, it'll be DI Martin thrusting out his chest in front of the cameras and getting all the kudos.'

'I've had my fill of being in the spotlight. And anyway, I've been around long enough to know that the same people patting me on the back will lay the blame at my door when things go pear-shaped.'

'You think they might do, then?'

'No idea. For sure, DI Martin has got a job on. There'll be vice-like pressure from above to get the whole thing wrapped up quickly.'

'Do you think it was suicide?'

'Until we have some hard evidence, it's just speculation.'

'Hazel doesn't think Steve would take his own life.'

'But it's clear she didn't know her husband as well as she—'

Matt was interrupted by the ringing of the phone down in his office. 'I'd better see who that is,' he said, hurrying away from her desk. Kate heard him answer, then moved closer so she could hear him better. The caller was shouting so loudly down the phone she could make out some of the conversation. She soon gathered that it was the errant councillor's wife and that she was not happy. In the middle of Matt's apology, the doorbell rang, startling the cat, who leapt from a chair near Kate's desk and hot-footed it into the kitchen.

She quickly made her way down the corridor to the front door of the building. When she opened the heavy oak door, Hazel was standing on the step. She was shivering and pale faced. Her eyes were wide and staring.

'Come in,' said Kate. 'Let's get you into the warm.' She led Hazel back through the inner door and into the main office. She could hear Matt talking on the phone in his office so asked Hazel to take a seat for a moment, while she made some tea. She noticed that Hazel's hand was trembling as she took the mug from her. They both sat in silence for a minute, sipping their drinks. Kate could hear that, annoyingly, Matt was still on the phone. She put down her tea and walked briskly down the room, put her head around Matt's open door and mouthed a message. 'It's Hazel.'

Matt signalled that he'd wind up the call. Kate hovered at the door until he finished and then asked Hazel to come through. Matt could see her agitated state as he gestured for her to sit down opposite him, with Kate at her side.

'I can see this is difficult for you. Could you talk us through what happened after we left?'

Hazel took a deep breath in through her nose and then puffed it out with a whooshing sound through her lips. 'The police took me to the river. The inspector told me to prepare myself for the worst… said there was a wound to his head. I was worried I might faint. When I got there, they'd put up a marquee near the riverbank. There was a boat there too, with divers. They looked like aliens in their big goggles and dripping wet suits. Inside the tent, I was introduced to a tall man with pale skin and ugly warts on his face. The body was laid out on a ground sheet, completely wrapped in polythene. The man pulled back the top of the covering for me to see his face. At first, I couldn't bear to look; I was shaking with the fear of what I was about to see.'

'You must be relieved it's over now,' said Matt.

'A relief… yes, it was at first. But then I thought… I still don't know where he is, if he's still alive.'

Matt raised his eyebrows. 'It wasn't Steve?'

'I knew right away it wasn't him. This man's nose was flatter, and his face was spotty. Steve has nice skin.'

'Did you notice anything else about him?' asked Kate.

'I don't know… the side of his head was a mess. I could feel my stomach churning, so I turned away as fast as I could to stop myself being sick.'

Matt was scratching the stubble on his chin. 'And the police, what did they say to you afterwards?'

Hazel frowned. 'DI Martin seemed disappointed. He asked me if I was sure, maybe the injuries had made him look different. Of course, I'm bloody sure…' she started to wail, 'does he think I don't know my own husband? He didn't even have the decency to apologise for putting me through all of this.' She looked up at Matt with pleading eyes. 'That's why I want *you* to carry on looking for him. Without you, we'd never have got this far.'

Matt fiddled with his shirtsleeve. 'I don't know if that is entirely true, but if you want us to, then of course we'll stay on the case,' he said, glancing over at Kate, who nodded her approval. He turned back to look Hazel in the eye. 'But, you know, we got a lucky break with the tie. Finding your husband could take a lot longer. We don't want to give you false hopes.'

Hazel's eyes welled with tears. 'But hope is all I have right now. Hope and blind faith.'

# EIGHTEEN

The Hand and Heart pub was just a short walk from his flat. Matt stood on the pavement outside and hesitated. A tension ran from his stomach and up into his chest. He was late and his brother Richard would be waiting for him. When he'd called his brother the day before to ask for help, Richard had suggested they meet there. It was one of Matt's haunts from his days in the force, but he hadn't been in for over three years. His last visit was etched clearly in his memory. It was the night before his whole world changed. He and DC Wallis had stopped off there on their way home to compare notes over a couple of pints. They were discussing their prime suspect, a certain Mel Toomey. After an operation spanning six months, they were getting nowhere. The next morning Matt had received an anonymous tip-off about a drugs deal going down in a house on Gregory Boulevard. He'd walked straight into the trap and been left for dead.

Matt made his way through the bar to the snug at the back of the pub. There, sitting alone in a dimly lit room, supping his pint, was Richard. The room gave off a supernatural vibe. It was in fact an ancient cave carved into the soft sandstone on which the city had originally been built. Richard got up to shake hands. 'I was beginning to wonder if you'd forgotten. Have a seat and I'll fetch you a drink.'

Matt was still feeling on edge as he sank into the hard wooden chair that was a little too narrow for his frame. 'Sorry, lost track of the time.'

'Apology accepted; what can I get you?'

'Pint of Best Bitter.'

Richard came back two minutes later, full glass in hand, and they toasted each other's health.

'How's life at the circus?' asked Matt with a grin.

His brother drew hard on his cigarette and puffed the smoke out again slowly through his lips before responding. 'You mean the war on drugs, prostitution and gambling? Getting harder by the day. Remind me, why the hell did we join?'

'No idea really. Mum was always dead against us following in Dad's footsteps. He did his best to put us off too. Must somehow be in our blood.'

'Do you miss it?' asked Richard.

Matt took a healthy sip of beer. 'In spite of everything, yes I do. Had no choice in the end, did I? Not that I blame the super; dug the hole myself.'

'I'm not so sure about that; if Dad were still with us, he'd be in awe of your bravery. Anyway, here we both are, and you've got your teeth stuck into a manhunt. Before

I go on, you do understand that this conversation never happened?'

Matt nodded. Richard stubbed his cigarette in the ashtray and pulled a ring-bound notepad from his jacket. He glanced around the room to check they were still alone before resuming.

'The police officer you wanted to talk to, Diane Collins, is stationed in Derby these days. Said she'd be happy to meet with you. I've written her home number down here.' Richard tore a strip from the page in his notebook and handed it to his younger brother.

Matt tucked the number into his wallet. 'Thanks for that. How did Diane react when you called her?'

'She's heard about Steve going missing but isn't confident she can be of much help. Either way, she's expecting your call.'

'What else did you get?'

Richard lowered his voice. 'Shouldn't be telling you this, but I bumped into DI Martin on my way out. The guy they pulled from the river earlier, it's now a murder inquiry.'

'Have they identified the body yet?'

'Last I heard, they were checking dental records.'

Matt paused. 'I have a hunch, but that's all it is. Could you see if the name Brian Henson, possibly living in the Beeston area, shows up on your records?' Matt then repeated the description Kate had given him earlier.

Richard looked over the brim of the glass he was about to sip from. 'Who is this guy?'

'Steve was due to meet him for a house viewing just before he went AWOL. We discovered that he gave a false address and phone number. So maybe that's not his real name either. Ring any bells?'

Richard put down his glass and leant back in his chair. 'No one comes to mind, but I can do a trawl in the morning, if you like?'

'Thanks, I owe you. By the way, do you know anything more about the search?'

'Only that they're focusing on the river and the woods nearby. But so far no more traces of your missing man. Just the tie.'

'Still early days. By the way, did you run that check on him for me?'

'I did. Your Mr Mackie was prosecuted for drink driving eight months ago and banned for a year.'

'Where was he stopped?'

'Victoria Street, early hours of the morning.'

'Any other offences?'

'No, that's the lot. Incidentally, he was three times over the limit.'

Matt paused to think. 'Victoria Street... that's where his club is. The Montague club.'

Richard gave him a knowing nod. 'We've busted that place once or twice.'

Matt raised his eyebrows. 'Oh really?'

'Yeah, late-night lock-ins. High stakes poker in the back room.'

'That's interesting. Find anyone I know?'

'The two guys that own the big taxi firm on Carlton Road. They had one of their mates with them – Michael Shanahan.'

'Shady Shanahan? Bloody hell, not him.'

'You two have history?'

Matt was looking over his brother's shoulder at the pit holes in the cave wall. He imagined he could see the outline of a pockmarked, snarling face. The same one he had glimpsed for an instant before the blade pierced his chest. Richard sensed his brother's anguish. 'Are you okay? Did you hear what I just said?'

'No, I mean yes… but it's not that. It's about the Steve Mackie case. I've been looking for a Geordie.'

'That narrows the search down to about half a million, then. Think Shady might be your man? Be careful if he brushes past you; got a big chip on his shoulder. Hasn't ever got over being muscled out of his home town. Where are you going with this?'

'It could just be coincidence, but a guy with a gruff Geordie accent phoned Steve's wife after he disappeared, anxious to find him. It might just be worth a friendly chat with my old buddy.'

Richard shook his head. 'I very much doubt it will be that; I'd tread very cautiously.'

'Fools rush in and all that?'

'I never suggested you were a—'

'So, just feeling protective of your little brother then?'

'Not really, but my glass seems to have run dry. Why don't you fetch us another?'

Matt gave him an apologetic look. 'I'm sorry, can we leave it till next time? I'm on late shift.'

'What's her name? Is it that pretty little assistant of yours?' asked Richard.

His face reddened. 'If you mean Kate, she's married. And even if she weren't, I don't make a habit of mixing business with pleasure. No, this is work. I've got a surveillance job to finish.'

\*\*\*

The sun was beginning to set by the time he'd parked his blue Beetle. Matt was sitting behind the wheel, his zoom lens camera on the passenger seat, hoping for another sighting of his target. The street was a row of well-maintained, grey-bricked semis with neatly tended front gardens. The councillor's wife had tipped him off that her husband would be on the prowl there tonight. The driver's window was wound down and Matt's eyes were trained on a house across the road with a green wooden gate. He could see into the living room, but there was no sign of life; he began to wonder if he'd arrived too late. Still, his meet-up with Richard had been worth it. Diane Collins had agreed to talk to him, and he'd found another person of interest in Michael Shanahan.

Since hearing mention of that name, Matt was on a trip back in time. The Dancing Magpie, as Shanahan's nightclub was named, was one of the places Toomey's dealers did their business. Matt still had a vivid picture of the night they raided it. Unannounced, his team had burst through the door of the back office. It was a dimly lit den, with an overpowering smell of cigar smoke. Sitting behind the desk counting the takings, as calm as you like, was a sharply dressed, handsome man with a chiselled chin and wavy black hair. He wore big, silver-framed sunglasses and a dark shaving shadow. 'And who might you be?' he had enquired in a deep, gritty voice, like some cool cowboy gunslinger. Instantly, he'd known it was going to take a lot to ruffle any feathers on Shady Shanahan.

A strong wind was getting up, whistling around his car. A young paperboy cycled past, then stopped and dismounted outside the house. He took a copy of the *Evening Post* from his weighty shoulder bag and pushed it through the letterbox. Soon after, Matt noticed shadowy movements in an upstairs window. Then a figure came into full view. A slender woman with jet-black, tousled hair, was clipping her bra together, both hands behind her back. Matt grabbed his camera and focused his zoom lens. A grey-haired man he recognised at once as the councillor came into shot; he put a hand on her shoulder and kissed her on the cheek. Matt pressed the shutter button in a series of rapid clicks. He put his camera down on his lap, let out a loud "whoop" and punched the steering wheel.

The car radio was on maximum volume for the drive back to his flat; the DJ was playing Roxy Music. The eerie vibrato of Bryan Ferry's voice brought back more memories of the raid on Shanahan's club. They were on their way out, walking around the dance floor towards the exit. He remembered "Love Is the Drug" blasting so loudly from the speakers that it made his eardrums vibrate. After all the meticulous preparations, he'd been left with nothing more than a loud buzzing in his head. That was when he'd begun to suspect there might be a leak from inside his own team. Shady had been just a little too cool, too laid back for his liking. Matt knew that his brother was right; his next visit to Mr Shanahan would need to be carefully planned and handled with caution.

Back at his flat he brewed himself a strong coffee and sat at the kitchen table. Supper could wait, but not his caffeine hit. Coffee, as far as he knew, was his only addiction. He didn't smoke and only drank too much alcohol when he felt low. And he'd never seen the point of gambling. He took a long sip from his mug and felt the tension in his stomach release. He decided to dictate his report on the wayward politician while it was still fresh in his mind. As Matt picked up his mini recorder, a plan formed in his head; it was about an upcoming interview he needed to record.

# DAY FIVE

Friday, 1 April 1983

# NINETEEN

Kate was on a mission her boss couldn't be involved in. Matt had briefed her on their person of interest, passed her a dossier to read for homework and wished her luck. Walking along Central Avenue in West Bridgford, she found the door she was looking for next to an Italian restaurant. She pressed the intercom, gave her name and was allowed in by an officious-sounding female voice. She climbed a steep flight of stairs and opened a half-glass door marked "Travers & Stevens, Accountants", which led to a carpeted reception area. Sitting behind the desk was a stony-faced, middle-aged lady in a pin-striped jacket, who reminded her of her headmistress at Nottingham High School. In a dismissive tone, she asked Kate to take a seat while she informed Mr Travers of her arrival, before slipping through an inner door.

While she was waiting, Kate picked up a travel

magazine from a coffee table. There were reviews of luxury holidays in exotic locations she'd scarcely heard of. Where, for heaven's sake, were the Turks and Caicos Islands? And Curacao? Wasn't that a liqueur? The glossy pictures, taken in bright sunlight, looked very alluring. Kate guessed they might just be the sort of places that Guy Travers would take Amanda to. Kate had only met Matt's ex-wife once; it was a long while back when she'd visited the office to bring some old clothes of his that she'd found in the back of a wardrobe. Amanda had stood in their main office, pointedly ignoring her, while she carried on a conversation with him as if Kate wasn't in the room. She wondered what Matt, or "Matty" as Amanda insisted on calling him, could have seen in her, apart from the obvious, that is. The sway of her slender hips that invited men to notice her, her perfect porcelain skin and her delicate face, framed by golden curls. Kate wondered why Amanda's eyes avoided her. *Is it true that the eyes are a window to the soul? If so, maybe she was afraid that I would see through hers and not like what I found.*

Her mental meanderings were interrupted by the click of the inner door opening. The formidable keeper of the gate had returned. 'Mr Travers will see you now – please come this way.'

Kate placed the brochure back on the pile and followed the receptionist through the door and along a wide but dark, oak-panelled corridor. Passing an open office, she spotted shelving units crammed with box files, filed company accounts and tax returns no doubt. The lady turned left through the second door, gesturing for Kate to go in, while she hovered by the entrance. Guy Travers got up from his chair to shake Kate's hand across the desk. His palm was clammy, and his handshake was weak and floppy. He was older than she had imagined, with well-groomed greying hair, neatly parted at the side, and round silver-rimmed glasses.

'Mrs Brooks, please take a chair. Would you care for a coffee, or tea?' His voice was as smooth as his polished desk. It reminded her of a BBC news announcer.

'Coffee is fine; white with two sugars,' replied Kate.

He nodded in the direction of his assistant, who turned on her heels and shut the door behind her, leaving them alone. After a few seconds of uncomfortable silence, Guy cleared his throat and spoke.

'I gather the police found the body of another man in the river close to where my client was last seen. I was taken aback when I heard, but frankly I don't think I can be of any help to you.'

'It's just a few routine questions.' Kate leant down to her briefcase and took out a notepad and pen which she placed on her lap. 'How well do you know Steve Mackie?'

'Quite well, I suppose. He's been my client for the past two years.'

'When were you last in contact with him?'

Travers stroked his smooth chin with a forefinger. 'Would have been about two months ago. He came here for some advice.'

'Can I ask what it was about?'

'A project he's involved in. He wanted my help in applying for a loan.'

Kate jotted on her pad before continuing. 'What did he need it for exactly?'

He paused for a moment. 'I suppose it's okay for me to tell you this. Mr Mackie is proposing to buy some land for a housing development.'

'Has his loan been approved?' asked Kate.

'Yes, it has. It was only when I tried to reach him to give him the good news that I found out he'd gone missing. Such a shock for his wife and fam—'

The door clicked open, and the receptionist came in with a tray and two coffees. She placed the mugs carefully on leather drink mats and left again. Travers took some sweeteners from a drawer and stirred them into his drink.

'Where was I?'

'The loan you arranged for Mr Mackie. By the way, how much is he borrowing?'

He raised his voice a touch. 'As I am sure you are aware, I'm not at liberty to divulge that.'

'Mrs Mackie is employing us to find her husband. Any information you have might help us to bring him home again.'

He looked down his nose at her. '*Mr* Mackie is my client, and I must put his interests first. I don't know the circumstances in which he left his wife.'

She took a sip of coffee; nice and strong, but not enough sugar. 'You think he's left her? Was there a problem between them?'

Travers sucked his cheeks in. 'If there was, he never mentioned it.'

'Have you met Hazel Mackie?'

'Only once, when she came here with Steve. They gave me the impression of being happily married.'

'Yet Mrs Mackie knew nothing about the loan you

arranged. Don't you find it odd that he didn't mention it to his wife?'

Travers shuffled in his chair. 'I suppose Mr Mackie must have his reasons.'

'Were you aware he'd remortgaged their house?'

He cleared his throat. 'I think he may have mentioned this, yes.'

'Mrs Mackie tells us she was unaware of this too.'

Travers fidgeted with his gold watch, which she noticed was a Rolex. 'I'm merely his accountant.'

*A very wealthy one at that*, thought Kate. 'How was his mood when you saw him last?'

'Very upbeat, I'd say. As I recall, we talked about sport. He's a keen rower and a big rugby fan. Likes the horses too. He grew up in Surrey, not far from Sandown Racecourse.'

'Likes a flutter on the races, does he?'

Travers smoothed his hair down with his fingers. 'I believe so. He's given me the odd tip, but I'm not really into betting. Accountants are not risk takers as a general rule.'

'I gather Steve belongs to the Montague club. They have a casino there, don't they?'

'Yes, we do.'

She tilted her head. 'You said *we*, you're a member too?'

'I am, yes.'

'What does Steve Mackie like to play? The roulette wheels? Blackjack maybe?'

'I don't think so. He prefers something more competitive.'

'What's that?'

'Rumour has it he's a pretty useful poker player.'

# TWENTY

Back at the office, Matt was downing a couple of aspirins with his coffee. Earlier, he'd woken in a cold sweat from a vivid dream. In it, he had slipped through a half-open door, past a steep flight of stairs and edged down a dark hallway. The muffled sound of conversation had come closer with each baby step. His face muscles had tensed as he stopped by a closed door, the voices now much louder. Poised to burst in, he was jumped on from behind. He felt two strong hands grab him around the neck. Regaining his balance, but still gasping for air, he had somehow wrestled himself free and turned on his attacker. He let out a gasp when he saw Guy Travers' contorted face. A split second later, a knife blade plunged into his chest, slicing through his skin. A shockwave of pain pulsed through his upper body and down into his legs. The imagined collision with the ground brought him back to waking consciousness and the overwhelming relief that this wasn't real, not this time at least. And it didn't take a psychoanalyst to work out why he'd seen Guy's face and not the real villain.

Taking another sip from his mug, he reflected on his morning. He had telephoned DS Diane Collins from his flat before breakfast and she'd agreed to meet him that evening at 7pm, after she came off duty. DS Collins had suggested the hotel opposite Derby railway station for their chat. The place would be busy, so nobody would be paying much attention to them. 'Should I carry a white carnation?' he'd suggested.

'No need for that,' Diane had replied, with a snigger. 'I can sniff out an ex-copper from a good mile away.'

Matt put the brown bottle of tablets back into the desk drawer and picked up his empty mug. On his way to the kitchen, the inner door opened, and Kate came striding through it. The cat jumped down from Kate's chair, stretched lazily and ambled towards her.

'And who's been sleeping on my chair?' said Kate, aiming an accusing eye at the ginger tom, who stopped in his tracks and looked up at her. 'I suppose you've left plenty of fur for me to sit on?'

Matt glanced down at his cat and, for the first time that morning, broke into a smile. 'Just keeping it warm for her, weren't you, Desmond?' Then he turned back to Kate. 'When you've taken off your coat and brushed your chair, I can't wait to hear what Mr Travers had to say for himself.'

Five minutes later in his office, Matt listened intently while Kate, reading from her notes, told him what had transpired at Guy Travers' office in fine detail. He was inwardly delighted to hear that she hadn't liked what she'd seen. She grimaced when describing his sweaty hands and his arrogant, posh persona. Matt let her give her report without interruption. Then he leant back in his chair, resting his elbows on the arms and clasping his fingers together.

'So, what conclusions have you drawn?' he asked, making strong eye contact.

'Number one, I don't trust Travers. My guess is he's closer to Steve than he makes out.'

'I agree, but we have no hard evidence to prove that, do we? And number two?'

'That Steve Mackie probably has some serious poker debts, which is why he's been asking friends to lend him money.'

'I think you may be right there, and there's more. An old pal of mine, Michael Shanahan, plays poker too. Heard of him?'

She paused for a moment. 'Can't say I have.'

'Shanahan came down from Newcastle a few years back. He owns the Dancing Magpie club. We became acquainted during a drugs raid there. Before you ask, we found nothing.'

A smile broke across her face. 'You think he's the Geordie who is so anxious to speak to Steve?'

'It's a distinct possibility. Let's talk more when I get back.'

She knitted her eyebrows. 'You're going out?'

'It feels a bit stuffy in here; thought I'd take a stroll down the embankment. Get some fresh air.'

***

Matt pulled up in his Beetle in the Water's Edge car park and walked towards the boathouse. A man fitting the description that Kate had given him came out of the afternoon shadows to greet him.

'Can I help at all?' asked the man.

'Mr Fletcher, I presume?'

'At your service. Please call me Eddie,' he said, shaking Matt's hand.

'Matt Crawford. My assistant Kate paid you a visit recently.'

Eddie scratched his forehead. 'Ah yes, you're the snoop looking for Steve Mackie. You think he's got something to do with the poor bloke they pulled out of the river?'

'Could be, we don't know yet. I leave it to the press to speculate. I've been given the task of finding him.'

'Isn't that down to the police?'

'Hazel Mackie has asked me to stay on the job.'

'And you're happy to take her money,' said Eddie, with a wry grin. ' I'm not sure I can be of any more help to you; told your assistant everything I know.'

'It's not you I'm after. Is Mrs Barton here today?'

'Linda? Yes, she is. Went out about half an hour ago. Should be back any time now. Why don't you go up to the bar and wait for her? I'll tell her you're here.'

Matt found his way upstairs and ordered a beer. There were just four others in the bar: a group of tracksuited oarsmen who had worked up quite a thirst judging by the battalion of empty bottles on their table. Matt had got halfway down his pint glass when the door swung open.

Linda Barton was still drying her blonde curls off with a towel as she walked towards him. He noticed four pairs of eyes following her athletic figure across the room.

'Mr Crawford, this is a pleasant surprise,' she said, with a smile that seemed overfriendly. 'Fletch said you wanted a word.'

He stood up and ushered her to a chair opposite. 'Looks to me like you could use a drink. What can I get you?'

She fluttered her long eyelashes. 'A lager and lime. Just a dash of lime, the barman knows how I like it.'

When he came back to the table two minutes later, Linda had draped the towel around her neck over a tight-fitting pink rowing vest. She took a sip of her lager and leant back in her chair. 'You have news of Steve? I was so relieved it wasn't him they found in the river.'

'Nothing new, I'm afraid. Are you missing him, Mrs Barton?'

Her face flushed. 'He's a good friend.'

'You've been seeing quite a lot of him, I hear.'

She blew out her cheeks. 'Who's been talking about us... bloody Fletch, it's him, isn't it?'

'Does Hazel know?' he asked.

'Know what?'

'That you've been shagging her husband,' said Matt, raising his eyebrows as he spoke.

She downed the rest of her drink in one, then wiped her mouth. 'No.'

'And your husband? Does he know?'

She fidgeted uncomfortably in her chair. 'Harry's never mentioned it. Anyway, it was only a couple of times.'

'And that doesn't count, I suppose,' said Matt, narrowing his eyes.

She shook her head. 'I'm not saying that. Anyway, it's never going to happen again.'

'What makes you say that?' he asked.

'I ended it. Last time we met up. He made a pass at me in the car, and I pushed him away. Told him we had to stop.'

'When was that?'

'Three weeks ago; I was giving him a lift home from here. A couple walking along the embankment saw us. Steve called me things I don't want to repeat, got out of the car and stormed off. I want you to know that I am totally ashamed of what I've done... you got a cigarette?'

'I've given them up.'

She got up from her chair, her hand trembling as she picked up her empty glass. 'Can I get you another one?'

'Think I've got time for a half,' said Matt glancing at his watch.

Linda came back with their drinks and a packet of Benson and Hedges. She peeled open the wrapper, took out a cigarette and lit up with a shiny gold lighter. 'You married, Mr Crawford?' she asked, blowing a smoke ring into the space between them.

He gave her a wry grin. 'Not anymore. Gave that up as a bad habit too. Sorry, that's not quite true. My ex-wife gave *me* the boot.'

Linda took a sip from her drink. 'I'm not using this as an excuse, but it's been hard since the accident.'

'I can see that. I'm not here to pass judgement. Hazel hired me to find her husband and that is my sole aim. Did

Steve ever mention anyone who was out to get him? An enemy perhaps, someone who he owed money to?'

She took a strong drag on her cigarette and tapped it on the side of the ashtray as she breathed out. 'I know he gambles a bit; fancies himself as a high roller. He's a popular guy, some might call him a likeable rogue. Can't say he's ever mentioned any enemies.'

'Has he ever asked you for money?'

She chuckled. 'No, it was strictly sex he wanted.'

'Does he talk much about work?' asked Matt.

'Yes, all the time.'

'Go on.'

'Lately it's all been about the big build in Stapleford. Says he's going to make his fortune. That's why I can't believe he's run away. Not now, it just doesn't add up. Something else must have happened, something bad.' She looked hesitant.

'What's on your mind?' he asked.

'Are you going to tell Hazel?'

Matt put his glass down and took a moment to consider her question. 'No, but I think she should know; it would be much better if you told her yourself. In the meantime, should Steve make contact with you, ring me at once.'

# TWENTY-ONE

The Dancing Magpie club was tucked away in a cobbled cul-de-sac in the Lace Market. As he approached on a deserted pavement, it seemed to Matt as if the street was taking a quiet late afternoon nap before another frantic Friday night. The double doors at the entrance were closed, so he pushed the button on a big antique doorbell to the side, took a step back and waited. After twenty seconds, one of the doors opened slowly, revealing a thick-set, bearded man with an indifferent stare.

'We don't open until 7pm,' he said in a flat voice.

'I'm here to see Mr Shanahan. I'm an old friend of his, Matt Crawford.'

The bouncer stepped forwards a pace and looked him up and down. 'How come I ain't seen you before?'

'I've not been round here for a while.'

'Why's that then?' he asked, flexing his fingers.

'Lost my job.'

'You looking for work?'

'No, I just need a quick word with Michael. Can you tell him I'm here?'

The big man stroked his beard. 'Wait here.'

Five minutes later, the door opened again. The man said nothing but ushered him inside and led him across the dance floor, the sound of his heavy shoes echoing around the empty room. They passed under a giant mirror ball, which hung from the ceiling, surrounded by spotlights. There was a smell of sweat mingled with stale smoke, and in one place, his feet stuck to the beer-stained carpet. They continued down a dingey corridor until they reached an open door. Matt's escort stood at the door and waved him into a long, narrow, windowless room, lit by a single light bulb dangling low from a crumbling ceiling.

At the end of the room, Michael Shanahan continued to read from the newspaper spread out on the desk in front of him for a few seconds before looking up. As Matt got closer, he saw it was the *Racing Post*. Matt heard the door click shut behind him. 'Mr Crawford, please have a seat.' Shanahan gestured to a rickety wooden chair, the sort you normally found in a spit and sawdust pub. It creaked as Matt cautiously lowered himself into it. 'Haven't seen you for a while. If you're still searching for my stash of hash, afraid your luck is out again.'

'I'm looking for a missing person.'

Shanahan gave a half-hearted shrug of his shoulders. 'Well, as far as I know, we don't have any of those on these premises right now. So, looks like you're all out of luck.'

'Let me be more specific. I am looking for a guy called Steve Mackie. Disappeared ten days ago. Know him?'

'Steve Mackie? The missing bloke in the papers. Friend of yours, is he?'

'No. I'm working for his wife.'

Shanahan's deep, throaty laugh turned into a cough. 'You… what?'

'I'm a private detective these days.'

'Really? Heard you'd had a nasty accident, mind. Suppose the police had no use for you afterwards?'

'Something like that. Let's get back to my missing person; have you seen him around?'

'Any reason I should have?'

'Steve likes a night out. Thought he might be one of your regulars.'

'Might be, but I've no way of checking. There's no membership here; we're not that kind of club.'

'Not like the Montague, then?'

Shanahan smirked. 'No, definitely not.'

'You know it, then?'

'Been a few times.'

'Steve Mackie's a member. I've heard he's a bit of a poker player too. I've got his photo here.' Matt pulled the Polaroid from his jacket pocket and placed it on the desk.

Shanahan looked indifferently at the holiday snap. 'No. Can't say I've ever set eyes on him before.'

'Certain?'

'Aye, quite certain.'

Acting out his despondency, Matt shook his head, got to his feet and picked up the photograph. 'Well, if he does show up—'

'I'll be sure to give you a shout,' said Shanahan, giving him an overfriendly smile. 'Now if that's the lot, Bruce will see you out.'

The bouncer was waiting in the corridor outside and had no doubt been keeping his ear to the door. The big guy led him at a slow plodding pace back to the front door. On the front step, Matt pulled his jacket collar up against the colder air and then walked slowly away down the quiet street. Although he saw no one and heard nothing but the buzz of city traffic, with the sixth sense of a professional observer, he knew there were eyes on him. He rounded the corner and saw the waiting Mini only fifty yards away, in a parking meter space. Reaching it, he opened the passenger door, got in and looked across at his assistant with a smile. She had been under instructions to come and find him if he didn't appear in an hour.

'All okay?' she asked.

'I think so,' he replied. He felt for something in his jacket pocket. As he pulled it out, the little black box was making a faint whirring sound. He held it in front of him, pressed the stop button and ejected the tape from the recorder. 'Says he doesn't know Steve. Let's see what Hazel has to say about that, shall we?'

# TWENTY-TWO

There was a Friday night buzz about the place that he liked. On approach the Midland Hotel was a grand affair: a three-storey red-brick building with large sash windows and a distinctive columned porch. The interior didn't quite live up to it. The decor looked tired, and the upholstery was worn and faded. He cast his eyes around the bar. A group of suited businessmen were putting the working week to bed with a Scotch or two on their way home. A young couple was cuddled up close in a corner, she sipping a Babycham, he with a half of lager. Matt had got there early and taken a table on the far side of the bar so that he could spot any arrivals by peering over the top of his *Evening Post*. Now and then, he turned a page to give the impression he was reading it.

Just as the hands of the large railway clock behind the bar moved to exactly 7pm, she appeared. She was just as

Richard had described her: curly dark hair cut above the collar and a pale complexion. He watched Diane enter the room with more of a flat-footed waddle than a walk. *Full marks for punctuality*, he thought. He watched her stop and glance around the room for a few seconds before looking in his direction. As their eyes met, she tilted her head, smiled and started to walk towards him.

'You wouldn't happen to be Mr Crawford by any chance?' she enquired as she hovered by his table.

He put down his paper and got to his feet. 'You found me. Was it that obvious?'

'To a trained eye, yes it was.'

'Pull up a chair and I'll get some drinks.'

She gave a little sigh as she settled into her seat. 'Don't mind admitting, I could murder a pint of lager.'

Two minutes later, he was back with their drinks. Hers had a frothy head, but his beer looked flat. He waited for her to swallow her first mouthful before continuing. 'Good day, then?'

She rolled her eyes. 'Don't even go there.'

'Okay, I promise. Why don't I start again? Thanks for agreeing to meet. No doubt my brother Richard explained a few things to you.'

'He told me that you're helping Hazel Mackie find Steve. I understand a man's body was found in the river near to where Steve was last seen.'

'That's correct. How well do you know Steve, by the way?'

She swept a dark curl of hair back behind her ear with her forefinger. 'We used to see quite a lot of him and Hazel. But since Carl…' Her voice trailed off.

'I know about Carl's accident.'

She paused to pinch the bridge of her nose. 'Moving here has helped; I needed a fresh start... I'm sorry, you didn't come here to talk about me. What is it you want to know?'

'How did Carl and Steve become friends?'

'Through Harry Barton. Harry and Steve belong to the same rowing club. Although Harry's rowing days ended after the crash.'

'Spinal injury I understand?'

She took a generous slug of lager and shook her head as she swallowed. 'I still hear a voice at the back of my head telling me that it was all my fault.'

'Really?'

'I should have said something when he told me he was driving into town. He told me they were getting a taxi home.'

Matt paused to take a mental note of what she'd just said. 'How often did they go on benders?'

'They used to meet at the Yates Wine Lodge on Fridays now and again.'

Matt was taken back to his youth: the double banks of wine barrels, sawdust for a carpet and the piano player upstairs, doing his best to break through the sound of raucous, alcohol-induced laughter. Matt took a sip from his glass. 'From what I know of Steve Mackie, doesn't strike me as the kind of place he'd want to be seen in.'

'He's moved up market since then; all part of his new persona of well-to-do businessman about town.'

Now Matt fixed her in the eye. 'What's your take on Steve?'

She shrugged her square shoulders. 'If I had to guess? He's got himself into trouble. With him it's either women or money, more than likely both.'

'You think he's seeing someone?'

'One or two if I were to guess.'

'Can you give me any names?'

'I don't know if—'

'Then let me run one by you: Linda Barton.'

'Not surprised. I think Steve's fancied her for a long time. She's got a roving eye too.'

'Anyone else you can think of?'

'No one comes to mind. She'd need to have money.'

'Likes digging for gold, does he?'

Diane nodded.

'How much do you think Hazel knows?' he asked.

'More than she lets on. I think she's been kidding herself for too long that he would change, that it would somehow fizzle out. If it were me, I'd have long since packed his bags for him and left them on the doorstep.'

Matt had no doubt she would have done; DS Diane Collins struck him as someone you wouldn't want to mess with.

***

Back in the flat, Matt was taking a last bite of cheese on toast and thinking that he'd been a little heavy with the Worcester sauce. He picked up his plate and took it to the kitchen sink, placing it next to a breakfast bowl encrusted with cornflakes. He filled his mug with over-brewed coffee from the machine and sauntered over to the sofa. Hard as he tried it didn't have the same rich taste as it did when Kate made it. Maybe it was the smile that came with it that made it better or the subtle smell of perfume on her skin as she leaned across him? He wondered what Kate would be doing now. She would probably be out with her old university friends in a wine bar or at the cinema. She'd mentioned wanting to go and see *Gandhi* at the Broadway. *I suppose I could ask her out*, he thought. *Wonder if there's space for me in her life? Maybe it's too soon; she's in the middle of a divorce and I don't know if I'm over Amanda yet. The scars she left me with are much deeper than the ones on my chest.*

Matt consigned himself to another Friday night in his own company. Even the cat had gone out on the prowl. His transistor radio was on a side table next to the sofa. He switched it on and flicked between stations for a while before giving up. There was too much going on inside his head to distract him. He was having thoughts about his conversation with Diane. What she had said confirmed the uneasy feeling he had about the Bartons. And what of Hazel? He wouldn't blame her for wishing to never see her husband again. Yet, here she was, prepared to forgive, and what's more, seemingly desperate to find him. Then there was Diane's lingering guilt over Carl's tragic accident. What was that all about? And last not least Carl himself; he had told Diane that he was getting a taxi home the night of the accident. *Wonder what made him change his mind?*

# DAY SIX

Saturday, 2 April 1983

# TWENTY-THREE

He was taking in the living room from the sofa while Hazel made them tea in her kitchen. There was a Cotswold stone fireplace with a long mantlepiece. In the centre was a colour photograph of Hazel the bride and Steve the groom standing on the church steps, in front of the tall stone cross of a war memorial. The keen-eyed detective recognised it at once as St Mary's in the Lace Market. He'd been there five years back for the funeral of a young constable who'd been killed in a motorbike chase. Hazel and Steve looked so incredibly young in the picture. She clutching a small posy of carnations and freesias and he with his arm around her waist and a boyish grin.

Just as he was studying an oil painting of a chestnut mare on the chimney breast, the latest version of Hazel appeared in the doorway with a tray and set it down on the low glass table in front of him. She poured a little milk into his teacup and then added tea from a matching blue china pot with a white floral design, before serving herself and settling into a facing armchair.

'You were lucky to catch me,' she said. 'I'm meeting Fiona Campbell in town in half an hour.'

'How is she?'

'Coping very well with being newly divorced and, thanks to you, she has no money worries either.'

It occurred to him that she had touched on a sensitive issue. 'How are you managing, money-wise I mean?'

'Mum and Dad are helping. Don't worry, your bills will be paid… is that why you're here?' she asked, clinking her teacup into the saucer.

'No, it's not. My fault, I should have explained right away. I want you to listen to a recording of an interview I did yesterday. See if you recognise the other voice.'

He took out his pocket recorder, put it on her side of the table, then pressed the play button. She listened in silence, staring at the wall behind him, to the dialogue between Matt and Michael Shanahan. When he clicked the stop button, she paused for a moment, then pointed her index finger at the recorder. 'That's the Geordie guy who rang asking for Steve.'

'You sure?'

She nodded. 'Yes, it's him. The deep, gravelly voice, the way he said "Mackie" with a soft "k" and that smoker's cough. How did you find him?'

'A bit of luck. His name came up in conversation.'

'Who is he?'

'Michael Shanahan. Mean anything to you?'

She paused for a second. 'No, nothing.'

'He owns the Dancing Magpie nightclub in town. Heard of it?'

'No, I haven't.'

'He says he doesn't know your husband.'

She clenched her jaw. 'Why is he not being straight with you? You think he's got something to do with Steve's disappearance?'

'Don't know, but I think they probably met at the Montague club – at a poker table. Mr Shanahan may have been calling in his debt.'

Hazel's nostrils were now distinctly flared. 'Steve? Poker? Who told you that?'

'His accountant, Guy Travers, mentioned it.'

She gave a deep sigh. 'It's all about contacts, Steve said. The Montague club's the place to be seen, he said.' Hazel shook her head. 'I had no idea about the poker games. You must think I'm a very silly woman.'

'No, I don't. Could just be you prefer to see the good in people.'

His words seemed to resonate; she looked at him with sad Labrador eyes. 'You mean, I'm too easily taken in?'

'When you love someone—'

She had a pained expression. 'I'm not sure if I do love him; I don't think I could ever trust him again. But I do still need to know what's happened to him. What are you planning to do next?'

'Some more digging into Mr Shanahan.'

'From what I've just heard, you'll need to be careful.'

Matt dismissed this with a shrug of the shoulders, although her concern for his welfare didn't go unnoticed. 'Have no fear, I will be,' he said, getting up from the settee.

'I'll keep you updated.'

'Think I'm becoming tired of sitting at home waiting for news. That's why I leapt at Fiona's invite for coffee. Linda Barton's coming too; haven't seen her for ages.' Hazel chewed on her lip. 'I'll see you to the door, and don't worry, I'll put your cheque in the post.'

\*\*\*

He was intending to go back home, get changed and find a pub on his way to the Forest game, but what Hazel had told him changed his plans. Her meeting with Linda was Matt's chance to speak to her husband Harry on his own. He drove across West Bridgford until he reached the playing field next to the Barton's bungalow. The approach road was filled with a long line of cars parked for Saturday morning football. Matt turned off and parked in a side street, then waited twenty minutes to allow ample time for Linda to leave.

As he opened the car door, he heard the shrill sound of a referee's whistle blowing and some derisive jeering from the crowd. Once he turned the corner onto the main road, the playing field full of muddy football pitches was in full view and the Bartons' bungalow was only a few paces away. He rang the bell and stood back from the porch. Thirty seconds later, he heard the clicking of the lock as the front door edged opened a few inches. A young girl with blonde, plaited hair poked her head around it.

'I'm Matt,' he said, 'Matt Crawford. Is your dad in?'

She took a small step out from behind the door in her

slippers and gave him a quizzical look. 'Does he know you?'

'Yes. I came to see him a few days ago. Can you tell him I'd just like a quick word?'

'Okay then, wait here.'

Two minutes later, she returned and led him via the hallway into the lounge at the back of the bungalow, where Harry was waiting in his wheelchair, looking out over the garden. He turned to his daughter. 'You can leave us to it, Zoe. Mum said you had homework to do.'

Zoe opened her mouth to speak, but then thought better of it. She nodded towards Matt as she left the room, closing the door behind her.

'A good girl, that one,' said Harry. 'Don't know where I'd be without her. Please sit down, Mr Crawford, take the comfy chair if you like.'

A copy of the *Daily Mail* lay on the easy chair Harry had pointed to. Matt picked it up and glanced at the headline. It was about the upcoming general election. 'Looks like Mrs Thatcher is good for another term then?' he said.

Harry blew out his cheeks. 'Yes, Northern Ireland's a bloody bomb site and we just fought a pointless war over a tiny island in the South Atlantic. But all that needless loss of life doesn't seem to matter to people; it does to me. Anyway, what's your news? Found him yet?'

Matt put the paper down on a side table and settled into the chair. 'No, not yet.'

'You think Steve had anything to do with the guy they pulled from the river?'

'They haven't identified him yet, but it's a distinct possibility. There's something I want to ask you, though.'

'Fire away.'

'It's about Carl Price. You two were obviously very close.'

'Carl was my best friend; we were at school together.'

'What was he like?'

'A bit like me, I suppose. We were different from the other kids; called ourselves the misfits. We preferred chess to football and model trains to girls. I think his mum was relieved about that. She had to bring him up on her own.'

'What happened to his dad?'

'He never knew his dad; his mum never married.'

Matt's eyes narrowed. 'You were going to be Carl's best man, I understand?'

'Yes, I was… and I know what you're thinking. Didn't do a very good job of looking after him, did I?'

'Diane Collins said something similar, about herself I mean, not about you.'

Harry's voice became high-pitched. 'You've spoken to her too?'

'Yes. She blames herself for what happened. She's never been able to work out why Carl got behind the wheel that night when he told her he was getting a taxi home.'

Harry began to blink rapidly. 'We… I… didn't realise how much he'd had. He was in a stinking mood that night. He called his mum from the pub, and Steve and I could hear him shouting at her. After he put the phone down, Steve tried calming him down, but it only made things worse. Then, he started having a go at Steve and it ended up with a scuffle and Steve pushing him across the room. Some chairs went flying, which got the landlord's attention. He asked us to leave.'

Matt sat forwards in his chair. 'Do you know what it was about? The argument with his mum?'

'I think it might have had something to do with Diane.'

'You mean his mum didn't like Diane?'

Harry's forehead wrinkled. 'Could be, I don't know.'

'What's his mum's name?'

'Ellie. Ellie Price.'

'Know where I can find her?'

'Haven't got her address, but I do know she's a devout Catholic. You could try asking at her church; it's the Holy Cross in Beeston.'

# TWENTY-FOUR

He felt a rapid drop in temperature as he entered the church. There was a faint smell of incense in the air as Matt walked down the stone floor of the centre aisle towards the altar. Standing there was a serious-looking young priest with wispy blonde hair who was holding a box of candles. When he saw Matt, he put the box down on the floor and started walking towards him.

'If it's Father Anthony you're looking for, he's taking confession.'

'No, it's not. I've come to see Mrs Price. Is she here?'

'The priest checked his watch. I think she'll still be in our meeting room; I'll take you there.'

He led Matt back along the aisle past the empty benches, the sound of their footsteps echoing loudly. Once outside, they took a short stone path laid in the grass to a new, red-brick building at the side of the church. They entered through double doors and passed along a corridor, leading to a large room with a pine floor. It reminded Matt of his old school gym. The sun was shining through the large picture windows, providing welcome warmth. At the far end of the room, three ladies were busy clearing dishes from trestle tables. As one of them was on her way to the kitchen armed with a pile of plates, the priest called to her.

'Ellie, there's a gentleman here to see you.'

'Be right back,' she called, without turning around. Matt heard a clatter of plates, and soon after, Ellie appeared at the door again, wiping her hands on her blue apron as she walked towards him. The young priest started to chat to the other ladies.

Ellie put both hands behind her neck to arrange her silky, dark hair, then looked Matt up and down. 'I don't think we've met. Did Father Anthony send you?' she asked in a sing-song voice.

He hesitated a moment, his gaze drawn to her full lips. 'No, he didn't. It's you I came to speak to Mrs Price. I'm Matt Crawford; Hazel Mackie has hired me to search for her missing husband Steve.'

She shuffled back a couple of steps. 'You're a private detective?'

'Yes. I understand you know Steve Mackie well.'

'Quite well,' she said with a distant stare. 'He and my son Carl were friends.'

'Is there somewhere we could have a chat?' asked Matt.

'Can this wait? I'm very busy at—'

The priest, who had clearly been listening in, came over to intervene. 'You're welcome to use my office, Ellie.

I can show this gentleman to my room while you are finishing up here.'

***

The office was a windowless space that looked more like a storeroom. Matt was taking it in while he waited for Ellie to arrive. There were cardboard boxes filled with prayer books and chairs stacked four high against the wall next to piles of hassocks. The room smelled of candlewax and mothballs. There was a solid oak desk against the far wall with a noticeboard above it. An events calendar pinned to it had been marked with a felt-tipped pen; charity teas, jumble sales, choir practices, prayer meetings and weddings had all been entered in a neat hand. All of this he noticed while his mind was still distracted. He couldn't take his thoughts off her soft, lilting voice and stunning Mediterranean looks. He knew instantly that Ellie was the Welsh voice on Steve's answerphone. And she fitted the description of the woman who Fabio had seen with Steve at the Montague club.

He heard her footsteps in the corridor before the door creaked open. He noted that Ellie had taken off her apron and brushed her hair. She wore a loose-fitting grey jumper and a long dark skirt. He pulled up a chair for her and she swept some fluff from her skirt as she sat down.

'I won't keep you a minute,' he said, taking a facing seat. 'It's just a few routine questions. How well do you know Steve?'

'He was a close friend of Carl's... my son's, that is. He was with him the night he died.'

'Yes, I'm sorry,' he said with an understanding nod. 'I did hear about their tragic accident.'

'It was three days before his wedding. We hadn't been getting on so well… we argued.'

'About what?'

She shook her head. 'I don't really remember… we could fall out over anything. For a long time after that, I blamed myself for Carl's accident.'

'But not anymore?'

'No, I'm through that now.' She stared down at her hands, which were crossed at the wrist on her lap. 'I didn't know where to turn when Carl died. Steve visited me after the funeral, and it became a regular thing. He was there for me; I put my trust in him. I suppose talking things through with Steve was my way of holding onto Carl.'

'How did Steve take Carl's death?'

'He said he missed him; he said he felt guilty that he'd survived and Carl hadn't.'

'He *said* he felt guilty, you said. Sounds like you're not sure if you believe him.'

She touched the cross on the silver necklace that hung over her blouse. 'I believe in God; I'm not certain if I have the same clarity when it comes to humanity.'

'When did you last see Steve?'

'About three weeks ago.'

'Can you be more precise?'

'I remember I'd been to a church meeting in the afternoon.' She looked across at the wall calendar to check the date. 'Yes, it was 14 March.'

'Where was that?'

'At the Rhinegold. We had dinner.'

'Nice place, was it a special occasion?'

'He'd had some good news about a building contract.'

Matt nodded. 'In Stapleford?'

'That's the one.'

'How did he seem that night?' asked Matt.

She sighed softly. 'Full of the joys. Like a schoolboy in a toy shop.'

'And you haven't seen him since?'

'No.'

'But you did try to contact him at the office a few days ago, didn't you?'

Her face flushed. 'Yes, I left him a message; he didn't return my call.'

'Can I ask why you rang him?'

She paused and folded her arms across her chest. 'I lent him a large sum of money which he promised he would pay—' She was interrupted by a rap on the door. A tall, strikingly handsome middle-aged priest in a black cassock entered the room and stopped in mid-stride.

'Ell… Mrs Price? My apologies for the intrusion.'

Ellie got to her feet and gestured towards Matt. 'Father Anthony, this is Mr Crawford. He's a private detective.'

The priest scratched his ear. 'Pleased to meet you, I'm sure. But what business might you have with us here?' he asked, in a lilting Irish brogue.

'I am making a few enquiries about a missing person.'

'A member of our congregation?'

'No. You may have heard about him, though. Steve Mackie?'

The priest lifted his thick, dark eyebrows. 'Yes, of course. I see now why you wish to speak to Mrs Price. I'll leave you in peace. If there should be anything I can help you with, I'm at your disposal.'

Father Anthony closed the door behind him and for a few seconds nothing was said. Ellie broke the silence, a tremble in her voice. 'Father knows too; he has been very... understanding. To be honest with you, I have been very foolish. I think my trust in Steve Mackie might have been misplaced.'

***

Two hours later, back in his flat, he and Desmond were together on the sofa, neither of them paying much attention to the game show on the TV. Matt was finishing off the can of Skol that had washed down his takeaway curry when he heard the phone ring. He sprang up, hurried to the hall and picked up the receiver. It was his brother.

'How's it going?' asked Richard.

'A bit too slowly, if I'm honest...' The line went dead for a moment, then he heard voices and a door closing. 'You still at work?'

'Just about to leave.'

'Got something for me?' asked Matt.

'You said you suspected that the man who Steve was supposed to meet, a Mr Brian Henson, might be the body we pulled out of the Trent.'

'Yes. Did you run that check on him?'

'I did but came up with a blank. Do you think that might not be his real name?' asked Richard.

'He did give a false address.'

'The man from the river has been identified as a Colin

Mason. Single, unemployed, twenty-eight years old with an address in Beeston. His mother told us his last job was at a nightclub. Guess which one?'

'The Dancing Magpie by any chance?'

'Right in one. Think this might be your Mr Henson?'

'Could be; Steve's secretary should be able to identify him. Her name's Monica Purvis.'

'I'll pass the info to DI Martin.'

'Good. I'll tell her to expect a call.'

Matt put the phone down and made his way back to the living room. On the TV, the ingratiating game show host was laughing at his own jokes, and on the settee, the cat was fully stretched out. Matt turned the programme off to allow himself space to think. Richard's news was a welcome step forward, but a cluster of unanswered questions remained.

What was Steve doing at the marina and who had killed Colin Mason? Shanahan was his key person of interest. Mason had previously worked for him, and Mackie owed him a pile of money. And why had Shanahan lied to Matt about knowing Steve? Then there was Harry Barton, who had reacted strangely to his questions about the night of the crash. Could he be holding something back? What about Ellie Price? What she had told Matt seemed to check out, but then he remembered what the barman Fabio had said about her intimate lunch with Steve at the Montague club. She'd freely admitted to loaning him a pile of money, but what, he wondered, was Steve's part of the deal? There was one thing he was certain about. If and when Steve did find his way home to Hazel, she would not be rolling out the red carpet.

# DAY SEVEN

Sunday, 3 April 1983

# TWENTY-FIVE

Matt had slept late and was woken by the cat meowing at the closed bedroom door. He'd climbed into his dressing gown and trailed Desmond into the kitchen. Then, after emptying the rest of a tin of Whiskas into a bowl, he'd tackled his own breakfast. Two strands of bacon fat and a slither of sausage skin were all that was left on the plate he'd pushed to one side. A fry-up was the best remedy he could think of for a troubled soul.

He was navigating his way through the voluminous *Sunday Times*, colour supplements and all. The front page carried a photograph of Arthur Scargill, NUM President, holding a megaphone to his mouth while addressing striking Yorkshire miners. Three million already out of work and the Government is threatening to close more pits. *Where will it end?* On the inside page, his eye was taken by a picture of people fleeing the scene of another terrorist bomb in Northern Ireland. *When will it end?*

Faced with the choice between staying home to read more depressing stories and going to his local, he decided to take what he considered the healthier option. He let the cat out into the garden, slipped on an old leather jacket and corduroy trousers and walked uphill in the direction of the Canning Circus roundabout. The Sir John Borlase pub soon came into view, perched high above the city. He ordered his usual pint of Shipstone's and was turning from the bar to look for a table when someone called out his name. 'Matty, good to see you.'

It was his ex-wife Amanda. She was standing chatting to two lady friends near the bar, cradling a large glass of red wine. She broke off her conversation with them and walked towards him in her patent leather high heels.

He forced a smile. 'Amanda. This is a surprise. Guy not with you?'

'Sunday's his golf day. I'm glad I bumped into you.'

'Really, why's that?'

'I was clearing out the spare bedroom the other day and found some old LPs of yours: David Bowie, Pink Floyd and Led Zeppelin. Do you want me to drop them round?'

'Sure, give me a ring when you're next in town.'

She looked at him with sudden focus. 'You okay, Matty?'

'I'm fine.'

She edged a little closer and gave him a thorough inspection. 'So, this is your new lived-in look, is it?'

He nodded slowly. 'Glad you noticed. It's taken a while to perfect.'

She tutted. 'You look like you slept in a dustbin, and you smell of tuna.'

'I'm flattered,' he said, taking a mouthful of beer.

'Guy mentioned that your assistant had been to see him.'

'That's right. Kate made an impression then?'

'Guy said she's pretty and smart.'

'Right on both counts; very perceptive, your boyfriend.'

She narrowed her eyes. 'Are you sleeping with her?'

His jaw stiffened. 'She works for me.'

Amanda shrugged her shoulders. 'Can't see what difference that makes. She's separated from her husband, I hear.'

'Have you been spying on me?'

'No, a friend at the tennis club mentioned it.'

'And did this friend suggest Kate and I were an item?' he asked. Amanda nodded in reply.

'It's idle gossip. For one, I'm not in the habit of sleeping with married women and two, as you well know, I never mix work and relationships.'

'Guy said that Kate was asking a lot of questions about one of his clients.'

'Steve Mackie. He's gone missing; his wife wants me to find him.'

'Quite a coup for you,' she said, tilting her glass to take a sip of wine. 'Getting a high-profile case like this. I wish you luck.'

'I might need it. Did Guy say anything else about Kate's visit?'

'I don't know if I should tell you,' she said, with a teasing grin.

'If it helps to find Steve Mackie, then you must.'

Amanda crinkled her nose. Her voice dropped to a whisper. 'You won't tell a soul I told you this?'

'Course not.'

'Guy's been pretty concerned about your missing man recently; apparently, he's up to his neck in debt. Thinks the poor man might have topped himself.'

\*\*\*

Several hours later, Matt was inspecting himself in the bedroom mirror to check if the tie he'd chosen went with the jacket. He was thinking about Amanda, when she used to shake her head at his choice and go the wardrobe and find the "perfect" one. It had to be pure silk. These days she was no doubt performing the same duty for Guy Travers. A man she walked out with had to look the business. In that respect, and in many others, Matt knew that he'd fallen well below the required standard. *Maybe I should have tried harder, been kinder to her friends, spent more time with her...* After a few more seconds lost in his thoughts, he decided the tie would pass. There were no visible food stains, even if it wasn't exactly the right colour.

His twenty-minute walk took him through Market Square and past the illuminated dome of the Council House. A group of skinhead youths was sitting on the steps under one of the arches. Each of them wore the same uniform: denim jacket, short jeans held up by braces and thick leather bovver boots. They were drinking out of cans and smoking roll-ups. The smell of strong tobacco wafted towards him on the wind. He crossed the road and continued uphill along Victoria Street until he reached the entrance to the Montague club. As he approached the front door, he could see that the ginger-haired man mountain was on patrol again. The bouncer stepped forwards to greet him.

'Good evening, sir. You a member?'

Matt affected an absent-minded smile. 'Gerry, isn't it? I was here last Tuesday to meet a friend. I think I left my umbrella in the bar.'

Gerry looked down at Matt and fixed him in the eye. 'You again; don't make this a habit. You've got ten minutes.'

The detective moved quickly up the steps and through to the stucco-ceilinged hall where the hostess made him sign in. He continued on towards the bar, walking past a table of overdressed diners discussing the evening menu over cocktails. Fabio was drying off some glasses as he approached.

'What can I get you, sir?'

'A half of *Carling*, Fabio. I'm in a hurry.' Matt passed him a five-pound note. 'Keep the change.'

Fabio poured his drink and placed it on the bar. 'Will there be anything else?'

Matt drew up a stool and leant closer, his voice dropping to a whisper. 'I was wondering if you know a friend of mine, Michael Shanahan?'

Fabio gave him an incredulous stare. 'You know Shanahan?'

'Yes, we are old buddies. Plays a bit of poker here, I understand?'

'I wouldn't know about that.'

'Are you sure? Ever seen him here with the guy I'm looking for?'

'Steve Mackie? Once or twice, yes.'

'Remember seeing anyone else with them?'

Fabio narrowed his eyes, as if struggling to recollect. 'I couldn't really say.'

'Maybe this will jog your memory.' Matt put a ten-pound note on the bar, which the barman slipped into his trouser pocket.

'Now I come to think harder, Mr Toomey might have been with them.'

'Mel Toomey?'

'Yes, that's right.'

Matt sat and stared into space for a few seconds. *Steve's involved with my nemesis.* He downed the rest of his lager and pushed the empty glass away. 'Thank you, Fabio. By the way, should anyone ask, you couldn't find my umbrella.'

The barman raised his left eyebrow. 'Pardon?'

'I told your friend out there I'd left it here the other night. Truth is, I didn't even have it with me.'

Fabio smiled, then raised his voice for the benefit of anyone listening in. 'Of course. Hope you find it soon, Mr Crawford. Sorry I couldn't help.'

***

His mind occupied with thoughts about Mel Toomey's connection with Steve, Matt noticed little around him on his brisk walk home. The light was beginning to fade as he fumbled for the keys, before fishing them out from under a handkerchief in his jacket pocket. He unlocked the main door, pushed hard and stepped inside the big hallway. As he closed it behind him, he saw a small white envelope lying on the doormat; it was addressed to Mr. M.G. Crawford and marked *Personal* in a hand he didn't recognise. He picked it up and held onto it as he made his way into the flat. He went from room to room, but there was no sign of Desmond anywhere; Matt guessed he'd probably exited through the cat flap for an evening prowl in the back garden. He put the letter on the kitchen table, then peeled off his jacket and loosened his tie before sitting down. He quickly tore the envelope open and found a note inside. The blue ink was smudged, and it looked hastily scribbled: *Matt, DI Martin wants me at the station. There's news about Steve. I think they've found him. Hazel.*

# DAY EIGHT

Monday, 4 April 1983

# TWENTY-SIX

The Crawford Agency, 9am: Kate was sitting opposite him, legs crossed, taking notes. He could see she was finding it hard to process the devastating news.

'Where did they find him?' she asked.

'In the woods by the river, downstream from the weir. The search party came across a small mound in the earth, which had been covered with fallen branches. The grave was shallow.'

'Do they know how he was killed?'

'He had multiple gunshot wounds.'

Her voice was strained. 'How is Hazel?'

Matt stroked his chin. 'She was strangely calm at the mortuary, almost cold.'

'Guess she's finding it hard to process. Maybe it doesn't seem real yet.'

'Not sure about that, but her thoughts have already

turned to finding his killer.'

'*Per Ardua ad Meta*,' she said.

He rolled his eyes. 'Did you just quote Latin at me?'

She chuckled. 'I assumed you, of all people, would know what it meant.'

He ran the words through his head again. 'Er... something about overcoming problems?'

'You're on the right lines. It translates as "through adversity to the goal". It's Hazel's rowing club motto.'

'She's a determined lady, that's for sure. In spite of my protestations, she's insisted we stay on the case.'

Kate ran her finger around the rim of her mug, then looked up at him. 'The gentleman doth protest too much, methinks.'

He rubbed his forehead. 'You still think I've got a thing for her, don't you?'

'Haven't you?'

'I make a point of never mixing business with pleasure.'

Kate gave him a cheeky grin. 'Never? I'll make a note of that.' She pretended to jot something down.

He felt a flush creeping across his cheeks. 'Look... we've got a murder case to solve, so let's focus on that, shall we? There's a lot more I need to update you on.'

Kate listened with increasing interest as Matt gave her the headlines on his meetings with Diane Collins, Ellie Price and Harry Barton.

When he'd finished, Kate did a quick scan of the notes she had made. 'What about the man in the river? Has he been identified?'

'His name's Colin Mason.'

'Otherwise known as Mr Henson, perhaps?'

'We'll have to wait and see; he did have a Beeston address. Monica Purvis is helping the police with that one, if she's up to it, that is.'

'You think he's somehow connected to Shanahan?'

'Possibly… or to Mel Toomey.'

Kate's mouth fell open. 'Toomey? That slime ball you nearly got killed for? You're joking.'

'Unfortunately not. I've discovered that he, Steve and Shanahan are, or rather were, poker friends.'

'You think Steve might have been killed because he owed them?'

'That's one line of thought, supported by the fact that Shanahan lied to me about not knowing Steve. Anyway, now I've brought you up to speed, what's your take on all of this?'

Kate put her pen down and uncrossed her legs. 'I think you're right to have Shanahan and his mates at the top of your list. But I get the feeling that the Bartons and Ellie Price should also be on our radar. Then we come to Hazel herself, do you believe she has been straight with us?'

He held out both hands, palms facing up in a "who knows?" gesture. 'Maybe not. Let's see what the coroner and the forensics team come up with; sometimes it's good to be guided by science.'

'Whatever happened to good old gut instinct?' she asked, with a shallow sigh.

He chuckled. 'Well currently, my gut is telling me I'm hungry. Fancy a bite to eat?'

\*\*\*

They were sitting in a small café in the Lace Market. It was Kate's favourite cake shop. The tables were tightly spaced, and it was incredibly loud in there, but the food was home-made, and the coffee was the best in town. Matt was munching on his last chunk of cheese sandwich when Kate pointed to his chest, grinned and told him that he had a smear of Branston pickle on his shirt. The little "tut" she let out as she said it reminded him of his mum. He picked up a serviette and wiped it away with a flourish, before folding the napkin into a neat triangle. Kate giggled at his play-acting and took another forkful of chocolate sponge. His appetite sated, Matt began to relax. Being with Kate made him feel that way too: calm and at one with the world. He had the sudden impulse to reach across the table and put his hand on hers, the way that couples do. But it didn't happen, even though he wanted it to. The sensible voice in his head reminded him of his golden rule, the one she'd just teased him about.

'Bumped into Amanda yesterday lunchtime,' he said.

Kate's eyes narrowed. 'That must have been a nice surprise; where were you?'

'I was in the Borlase having a quiet drink. She was there with a couple of girlfriends. We didn't talk long.'

'How is she?'

'Very interested in you since your chat with her boyfriend. I reckon he's taken a fancy to you.'

She coughed. 'I can assure you the feeling is not mutual. She has no call to be jealous.'

Matt sipped on his coffee, then winced. It had gone cold. 'I've been thinking about what you said earlier. Maybe you're right, we shouldn't just sit back and wait for the police reports.'

Her eyes lit up. 'What's next then?'

'There's something I'd like you to take care of. I think that Ellie Price would be more comfortable speaking with another woman. I'd like you to call on her. Do a bit of gentle probing about her friendship with Steve and see what she has to say about Hazel. I don't believe her story about not remembering what she and Carl argued about the night he was killed. Her last words to her son would surely be imprinted on a mother's memory for all time.'

'And you? What are your plans?' she asked.

He drew in a deep breath. 'Me? I'm in the mood for dancing.'

She froze, her ham sandwich held in mid-air. 'Am I imagining it, or did you just quote the Nolan Sisters?'

'At least it's not Shakespeare or bloody Latin!'

She chuckled. 'Well amen to that.'

# TWENTY-SEVEN

Matt arrived early evening at the Dancing Magpie dressed in his Levi's and black leather jacket. He joined a small queue at the bar and, while waiting, carefully scanned the dancehall. He couldn't see the auspicious owner lurking anywhere. The tall barmaid had short, spikey black hair and wore a studded leather collar around her neck. She was weirdly attractive, although he wasn't sold on her heavy orange face make-up. When he got closer, he could see that beneath it, her cheeks were pockmarked. He ordered a large scotch on the rocks. Avoiding eye contact, she picked a glass from a low shelf and pushed it up into the whisky dispenser. She clunked his drink heavily on the counter and it was as she reached for the ice bucket that he saw it: the unmistakable inking on her right forearm. The ornate black Celtic cross, accentuated with scrolls and arrow-like points. It was the very last thing he remembered seeing before the blade went in. There was a ripple of tension building up in his chest and an inner voice told him to slow down and take measured breaths.

His tone was as casual as it could be when his insides were churning. 'One cube's enough, thank you.' There was a clink of ice on glass, then she slid the drink across the counter, and he paid. As she was pressing the change into his palm, Matt asked if Mr Shanahan was there.

She scratched her forehead and puffed out her cheeks. 'I'll have to check. Sorry, who are you?'

He suspected she knew that already. 'I'm Matt Crawford, a friend of his.'

'Is he expecting you? Only he don't speak to salesmen. You'll need to ring for an appointment, so you will.'

'I'm not selling anything; just let him know I'm here, please.'

Matt picked up his glass, took a swig and told her he'd wait in a booth over on the other side of the dance floor.

An inch of whisky later, the tall figure of Shanahan appeared from the gloom of the low lights. He ambled towards Matt's table and sat down opposite him.

'Back so soon? You must like it here.'

Matt looked down at his glass. 'The Scotch is okay; I'll give you that. But that's not why I came back.'

Shanahan gave him a surly smile. 'Really? Then why?'

'I need you to level with me.'

'About what?'

'About Steve Mackie. You play poker with him, I hear?'

Shanahan creased his nose. 'Look, here's the thing. I play poker with a lot of people. Where's this going, pal?'

'Steve Mackie is dead. He was shot.'

Shanahan's mouth fell open and he touched his bottom lip as he spoke. 'I'm sorry to hear that. But what's this got to do with me?'

'He owed you money, didn't he?'

The nightclub owner's jaw stiffened. 'What if he did? You really think I'd be that stupid?'

Matt stared him down. 'As I said, I just want the truth.'

Three seconds of silence. 'Okay, he owed me money.'

'How much?'

'Three grand.'

'And you were okay with this?'

'Not exactly, but I wouldn't... I didn't kill the guy.'

'Any idea who might have?'

Shanahan shook his head slowly from side to side. 'Asking me to do your job for you now? I've no bloody clue.'

'Does he... did he owe money to anyone else? Your friend Mel Toomey for instance?'

'You'll need to ask Mel about that.'

Matt pursed his lips. 'Maybe I will.'

\*\*\*

Matt stepped out of the club into a cool evening breeze and dark clouds gathering over the city skyline. He walked to the end of the cul-de-sac and turned left, heading downhill in the direction of the Market Square. He checked his watch as he approached the taxi rank to see he was running late. He jumped into a black cab. The king-sized, sullen-faced driver was devoid of conversation, allowing random thoughts to occupy Matt during the ride across town. The image of the Celtic cross still lingered in his head. He had no doubt that the tattoo belonged to the woman who'd knifed him. He would soon find out who she was, but then what? It was her word against his. Shanahan had seemed genuinely surprised about Steve's murder, but that might be a poker player's bluff. And what of Hazel? Her reaction to her husband's death had been unexpectedly cool. He didn't want to think it was her. *It couldn't be her, could it?* If it was, he had been duped, with all the consequences that would bring. The story would be all over the papers and the bad publicity might bring the agency down. Maybe he would get nearer the truth tonight.

The taxi turned left after Trent Bridge and dropped him on Bridgford Road. From there it was a short walk to the Manor House pub. The pub was a large, red-bricked building with cream Georgian windows which might have been mistaken for someone's residence, but for the sign on the front wall. He had taken Amanda there once when they first met. It was just the once, before he discovered she was more comfortable in wine bars. The wine bars he could pass on, but sometimes, alone in bed at night, he did miss the soft feel of her skin.

Matt steered his way through clutches of drinkers at the bar, but there was no sign of her. As the room opened out in front of him and space appeared, he saw her sitting at a small table on the far side of the lounge, cradling a large glass of white wine. Fiona looked stunning, her dark curls falling over a low-necked black pullover. *Being single looks good on her*, he thought. As he got closer, she waved at him, got up from her chair and gave him a close hug.

So close that he felt her ample breasts pressing against his chest.

Trying, but failing, to hide how much she had aroused him, he slipped out of her embrace. 'Ex… cuse the late arrival. It's been one of those days.'

She touched his shoulder, picking some imaginary fluff from his jacket. 'Yes, I can smell it on your breath. Why don't you get yourself another? Mine's a Chardonnay.'

Five minutes later he was back at the table with their drinks. He sat facing her and glanced around to check on any eavesdroppers; nobody caught his observant eye, but nevertheless he spoke in little more than a whisper.

'Heard any more from Hazel?' he asked.

'Not since last night. You needn't worry about her, darling, she's going to be absolutely fine.'

Matt connected with her soft amber eyes. 'What makes you say that?'

'Hazel is strong,' she said, leaning in closer. As she did so, Matt picked up the scent of wild flowers.

'How were Hazel and Steve getting on when he went missing?' he asked.

Fiona hesitated for a moment. 'Things hadn't been great between them for quite a while. But I think I might have made it worse.'

'Really? In what way?'

She sipped on her drink and winced. 'It's still a bit cold for me. Sorry, yes, you were saying?'

'You think you may have upset their marriage?'

'I shouldn't have said anything.'

'You know that what you say to me goes no further,' he said earnestly.

She laughed. 'I didn't mean that. I meant that I shouldn't have said anything to Hazel.'

'About what?'

'I saw Steve having dinner with another woman. They were holding hands across the table and gazing fondly into each other's eyes.'

'When was this, exactly?'

'Three weeks ago. I was with my friend in the Rhinegold. It was her birthday, 14 March. I don't think he saw me.'

'Did you recognise the lady he was with?'

'Couldn't believe it at first; it was Carl's mum, Ellie Price.'

'And you told Hazel what you had seen?'

'Yes, when we met for coffee two days later. She burst into tears; everyone in the place had their eyes on our table. I'm not very good at knowing the right thing to say, but I had to tell her. What that deceiving bastard Philip did to me over all those years, I didn't want that for her.'

'You were right to tell her. Do you know what she did afterwards?'

'You mean, did she confront Steve with it? I don't know. When she calmed down, she thanked me for telling her. There was a steeliness in her eyes I hadn't seen before. We haven't spoken about it since.'

Matt felt her eyes on him as he drained his glass.

'Let me get us another,' she said, getting up from her chair and adjusting the short, pleated skirt she wore over her black tights.

Matt felt a sudden surge of heat through his body as he rose from his seat. 'It's very kind of you, but I think I've had my fill.'

She stepped closer and stroked his arm; he had a tingling at the back of his neck. 'How about a coffee then? My place is not far.'

He followed her out of the pub and onto the street. Fiona linked her arm through his and leant her head on his shoulder as they strolled along the pavement under the street lights. On the edge of his vision, he saw a man, hands in pockets, shuffling out of the shadows across the road, heading in the same direction.

# TWENTY-EIGHT

Central Police Station, 10pm: DI Joe Martin and his protégé DS Andy Crowther were alone in the incident room. Joe had taken Andy under his wing when the young man had joined the force seven years ago. Joe knew early on he'd found an ideal partner. Unlike himself, Andy was studious and very methodical. He found books easier to read than people and spent his spare time searching second-hand bookshops to add to the shelves in his flat. Local history was his specialist subject.

The two officers stood three feet apart, staring at the blackboard. The only sound was the loud ticking of the wall clock. The board had been plastered with photographs; the connecting lines between them made it look like a family tree. At the top were pictures of the two victims: Steve Mackie and Colin Mason. They had the grainy quality of enlarged passport photos. Under every picture was a name and, in some cases, a cryptic note or a question mark. Joe Martin sighed, then turned his head towards his DS.

'What a bloody mess. Two men down, no murder weapons, no motive, no witnesses and a private eye running rings around us. What's your take on it, lad?'

The DS adjusted his bottle-thick, gold-rimmed glasses, which had slid down his nose. 'What's interesting me is the difference between the two killings. Colin Mason was clubbed to the head whereas Steve Mackie was shot.'

'Suggesting what?' asked Joe. 'That we might be looking for two killers, not one?'

'Too early to say. We need to find the murder weapons.'

'Any evidence at all would be a start,' said the DI with a grunt.

The DS rolled his eyes. 'The blood we found on the rocks by the river is from a rarer blood group, A negative. It's the same as Colin Mason's. Then there's the blue transit the neighbour saw.'

'Got any further with that yet?'

'There's nothing registered to Colin Mason. I've got the guys doing stolen vehicle checks.'

'Okay, let's look at what we know so far.' The DI pointed towards the picture board. 'Colin Mason, using the name Brian Henson, got Steve Mackie to meet him at a house on Meadow Road that afternoon. Why would he do that and why choose this property?'

'Colin was unemployed and living off benefits. He was in no position to buy the house,' said Andy. 'He chose it because he knew it was empty and so it would be an accompanied viewing.'

'I'd got that far too. Any further thoughts?' asked Joe.

'Could be he was paid to play the role of house buyer by someone wanting to lure Steve there. Or, just possibly, he had a grudge to settle himself.'

'Maybe Shanahan hired him; he used to work for him after all. I want you and your team to speak to Mason's family, his neighbours, other former employers. Let's see if he had any connection with Steve Mackie. And let's find out who his friends were, where he drank and if he was in anyone's pay.'

'You think he might have been hired as bait and then thrown back into the river when he'd done his job?'

Joe smiled. 'Nice imagery. Yes, that's one possibility. See what you can dig up, sorry, I mean fish out.'

'Will do,' said Andy with a wry grin. 'Shall we move on to Steve Mackie?'

'Here we know more. Shot in the back multiple times with 19mm calibre bullets fired from a Browning Hi-Power semi-automatic pistol. The wounds indicate the range was between twenty and thirty yards.'

'Running away from his captors?'

'More than likely,' said Joe. 'But who were they? What reason did they have for wanting him dead?'

'We know he owed big money to Michael Shanahan,' said Andy, running fingers through his hair. 'But he isn't the only one on our list. Maybe Shanahan or one of the others ran out of patience.'

'Okay, so let's look into all of the people he was in debt to, business and personal debts. Get someone to call at his office and go through the books. Let's talk to his wife again and see what she knows.'

Andy turned his head to make eye contact with his boss. 'What's your take on Hazel Mackie?'

'Hazel interests me. She's hired a private investigator. A bit over the top, wouldn't you say? Unless of course you wanted to create the impression that you would do anything you could to find your loved one and shift suspicion away from yourself. And there's one more thing. Did you notice her reaction at the mortuary?'

'Not really, if I'm honest,' said Andy.

'That's exactly it – there was none. A complete lack of emotion. Strange, don't you think?'

'Suppose so. Perhaps she was numb with shock.'

'Or maybe it's all a front to hide the fact that she couldn't stand the sight of him. She's already told us he'd taken out loans without telling her. I wonder what else he kept secret from her?'

'It's true she has no alibi for the night in question. She told us she was at home alone waiting for him to come back.'

'And she didn't report him missing until the afternoon of the next day.'

'That's not so unusual. Maybe she thought he'd stayed over with a friend?'

'But you do see why I've still got her in the frame?'

'I suppose you're going to quote statistics about the murderer most often being someone close or known to the victim?' said Andy.

DI Martin smiled ruefully. 'I'd be wasting my time; you already know them.'

'You're right. Eighty per cent of murderers are acquainted with the victim.'

'And what portion is family?'

'Twenty per cent.'

'I might dispute that, but let's move on. There is one more line of inquiry I'd like you to follow.'

'What's that?'

'If Colin Mason was muscle for hire, then the killer might well be a gun for hire. Who would have enough money to pay a hitman? See if any of our informants has heard anything on the street about a contract on Steve Mackie's head. Let's invite our Mr Shanahan down here for a chat too. It's about time we started setting the pace on this murder inquiry, not Matt bloody Crawford.'

# DAY NINE

Tuesday, 5 April 1983

# TWENTY-NINE

The Crawford Agency, 9am: Matt had just finished bringing Kate up to speed on his visit to the Dancing Magpie and his evening with Fiona Campbell. When he told her that he thought he was being followed, Kate questioned whether he was just being jumpy. 'Of course, I was jumpy – I'd just seen the woman who stabbed me,' he'd said in a raised voice. Inwardly, Matt realised that she may well be right. Naturally, he omitted a number of "trivial" details, such as where he had spent the night, who with and what she had made him for breakfast. He'd done his best to convince himself that sleeping with Fiona had no bearing on the case, even though he realised there might be consequences.

There was another reason for his feeling edgy. He had broken his golden rule: "Never mix business with pleasure". A pleasure it had definitely been though; the very best kind of therapy. He closed his eyes, took a slow breath in. A video of last night in Fiona's bedroom played in his head. When he opened them again, his vision of Fiona had transformed into Kate, her arms folded across her chest.

'Matt, did you hear what I said?'

'I'm sorry... what?'

'I said it's odd that Hazel didn't say anything about Steve's affair with Ellie Price.'

'Yes, very odd; she must surely have recognised Ellie's voice when we played her the recording. I'm going to call on Hazel to get her version of events. I want you to hold fire on your chat with Ellie until I've done that.'

She nodded her approval. 'Okay, makes sense. So, what about Shanahan's barmaid? Do you want me to do some follow-up on her?'

'You can put a few feelers out if you like; find out who she is and where she hangs out. But I don't want you paying her any visits, you understand? It's too dangerous.'

\*\*\*

Matt was taking in the room while Hazel made tea. His sharp eyes saw that her wedding photo had gone from the oak mantelpiece. It had been displaced by a row of condolence cards. Most of them looked alike: bunches of pink or purple flowers and messages like "With Deepest Sympathy" or "Thinking of You". One of them stood out from the crowd: a night scene where one star shone brighter than the others. It had the words "ONE MORE STAR IN THE SKY". His curiosity stimulated, he took a quick peek inside and saw it was simply signed, *With love, Monica xx*. Matt wondered how Steve's secretary was holding up. Probably not as well as his client, he thought, as he heard Hazel pattering down the hallway with their drinks.

Hazel hovered over the carpet with light, graceful steps. She leant forwards to pour their drinks through a strainer from a white china pot, then settled in an armchair facing Matt, her legs crossed at her ankles. He couldn't help noticing how shapely they were until he reminded himself of his first rule of engagement and averted his eye. She leaned back in her chair and waited for him to speak.

'How are you coping with all of the hullabaloo?' he asked, before sipping on his hot tea.

'You mean the press hanging around outside? It's a bit weird, actually. I'm not used to all this fuss. You said you had some news?' she asked, tilting her head to the side.

'Yes. We've been able to identify the person on the recording I played you.'

Hazel choked on her tea. 'Oh… have you?'

Matt pretended not to notice. 'We have. It's a lady called Ellie Price.'

Her face flushed deep pink. 'Ellie… who?'

'Come on, Hazel, you know exactly who. She is Carl's mother. What's more, she was having an affair with your husband, wasn't she?'

'Did she tell you that?'

Matt didn't deny it; Hazel didn't need to know it was Fiona who'd told him. He continued his probing. 'I'm a little confused. You know her well, yet you said you didn't recognise her voice.'

Hazel looked down at the floor, not knowing what to say. Matt put his cup down with a shake of the head. 'Look, Hazel, if you want me to work for you, you need to be straight with me.'

She took several quick breaths. 'I'm sorry. I couldn't… I can't.'

'Then *I'm* sorry too, but I can't help you anymore,' he said, getting up to leave.

'Don't go,' she pleaded, looking up at him, tears welling in her eyes.

Matt hesitated, then sat down again, waiting for her to calm herself.

She took a tissue from a box and dabbed her eyes. 'Okay, okay, I'll tell you why. But before I do, you must know I was only protecting him.'

'Protecting who?'

'Steve… and Harry.'

He leant closer to her. 'Protecting them from whom, from what?'

She was blinking more tears away as she made eye contact again. 'I couldn't tell you about Ellie, because I thought you might suspect something and talk her into revealing the truth.'

'About what, exactly?'

'The accident. Steve and Harry lied to the police. Steve was driving the car that night, not Carl.'

# THIRTY

Half an hour later, still digesting what Hazel had told him, Matt had driven across West Bridgford to Mackie Estates and was sitting with Monica in her late boss's office. The photograph of the agency opening still hung on the wall: Monica in her trouser suit and Steve in his blazer and favourite floral tie. The tie that Matt had spotted at the marina, the tie that would now no doubt be sitting inside an evidence bag.

Matt noticed a change in Monica; her forehead was creased, and she was fidgeting with her silver neck chain. 'How are things here?' he asked.

Monica pointed through the glass partition to the main office, whose solitary occupant was her assistant. The young ginger-haired girl was opening the post. Sensing their eyes on her, she paused to give them a shy smile. 'As you see, we are not busy. It seems the news about Steve has frightened people off. Two clients have cancelled on me this morning.'

'I'm sorry to hear that,' said Matt, with a rueful shake of the head. 'Hopefully, it will all settle down in time. People have short memories. Have the press been bothering you?'

'We had a bunch of reporters hanging around outside yesterday. It was putting customers off coming in, so I went out to them and told them I had nothing to say. Haven't seen them since.'

'Good for you. And what's the news from the police? Did they get in touch after I rang on Saturday? Have you been to the mortuary?'

The corner of her mouth trembled. 'S… sorry, I promised to let you know, didn't I? D… DI Martin was very kind. He picked me up Sunday evening. I'd worked myself into a bit of a state; I've never seen a dead body before. The room was cold and smelled of chemicals. I was starting to feel queasy, so I asked them to get a move on. When they pulled the curtain back, he was lying there, all alone, so utterly still. My head felt light, and I couldn't focus my eyes at first… it was horrible.' Tears started to well up in her eyes.

'Did you recognise him?'

She cleared her throat. 'Yes, it's him – Henson – although DI Martin told me later that it's not his real name.'

'That's right,' said Matt, letting out a heavy sigh. 'His real name is Colin Mason, and we suspect he had little interest in buying a house.'

Monica took off her glasses and wiped her eyes with a handkerchief. 'You think Mason was used to lure Steve there?'

'Yes, I do,' said Matt, thoughtfully brushing his chin. 'Monica, I need you to be very straight with me. Can you think of anyone who might have wanted to do Steve harm?'

Monica was blinking rapidly as she replaced her glasses. 'No, I can't.'

Matt looked her in the eye. 'Does the name Mel Toomey mean anything to you?'

'No, nothing.'

'You sure about that? He and Steve were friends.'

'I'm sure.'

Matt paused for a moment. 'I need to ask you this. Did Steve do drugs? Did he deal drugs?'

Her jaw stiffened. 'Steve? He would never do anything like that.'

'Then let me ask you about someone else. Do you know a lady called Ellie Price?'

'I know the name. She's Carl Price's mum. He and Steve were good friends.'

'That's right. Do you know what? Hers was the voice on the answerphone message you found.'

She leaned back in her chair. 'As I just said, I never met her.'

'Turns out that Steve crashed the car that killed her son, Carl.'

Monica's mouth gaped open. 'But… Steve said—'

Matt raised his palm to interrupt. 'I know, Steve said he was a passenger. He was lying, about that and many other things, I'm afraid.'

# THIRTY-ONE

The Dancing Magpie, 8pm: Michael Shanahan was at his desk in the back office totting up the takings on his calculator when he heard a knock on the door.

'What do you want?' barked Shanahan.

'It's Bruce, Mr Shanahan. There's someone to see you.'

'Not now, mate, I'm busy.'

'It's Mr Toomey, boss.'

Shanahan sighed. 'Okay, show him in.'

The door opened slowly and Bruce, the bear-like doorman, shuffled in, followed by a sharply dressed older man with slicked-back white hair and big glasses with a blue tint. He wore a dark blue suit with a pink shirt, open at the neck to show off a heavy gold chain. Shanahan signalled for Bruce to leave them, and when the door closed, he got up and shook hands across the table with his friend, gesturing for him to take a seat.

'Like a Scotch?' asked Shanahan.

'What you got?' asked Toomey.

'Glenfiddich.'

'In that case, yes.'

Shanahan opened the door of a cupboard behind his desk, taking out two tumblers, then a bottle. He set the glasses on the desk and poured two inches of malt whisky into each of them.

'Your good health,' said Shanahan, meeting his friend's eye and taking a generous slug. 'What can I do for you?'

Toomey's eyes narrowed. 'Heard that our old friend Crawford paid you a visit the other night.'

'I suppose Tamara told you?' said Shanahan.

'She did mention it, yes. How is Crawford?'

'Not in great shape. We both know why.'

Toomey took another sip of his drink and smacked his lips, relishing the taste. 'He should be more careful.'

Shanahan offered him a cigar from a wooden box on the desk. Toomey declined, but Shanahan took his own, snipped the end with a knife and lit up from a silver lighter while his friend continued.

'Tammy don't have much time for the police on account of what happened to her dad. How's she settling in here?'

Shanahan slowly blew out a plume of cigar smoke. 'No complaints so far.'

'Good. What did Crawford want? Tamara's a bit spooked. She thinks he might have recognised her.'

'No, her name didn't come up. He was asking about Mackie, if he owed me money.'

'Did you tell him?'

'Yes, I did.'

'Which puts you right up at the top of his list.'

'Maybe it does, but believe me, I didn't kill him, Mel. He must have owed you too?'

Toomey bit his lip. 'Yep. Just short of five grand. Told him it could wait.'

'That doesn't sound like you, Mel.'

'I made an exception with Mackie. Admittedly, the guy was a bit of a prick, but I couldn't help liking him.'

'Must admit, I was surprised you got into business with him.'

'My accountant suggested property. He said something about widening my portfolio. Whatever you think about Steve, he had good contacts.'

'You mean he greased the right palms?'

Toomey gave a throaty chuckle. 'It's a sound investment, can't fail.'

*And now he's dead you can muscle in and take the lion's share of the profits too*, thought Shanahan before continuing. 'What do you think happened to Mackie?'

'I dunno. Maybe he pushed his luck too far. Could be someone put a contract out on him.'

'Any ideas who?' asked Shanahan, eyebrows raised.

'No one's put their hand up and there's no noise on the street.'

'Heard how the police are doing?'

'All I've heard is Joe Martin's on the case with a young DS, still wet behind the ears.'

'Joe Martin. Is he the guy who arrested you a while back?' asked Shanahan.

'Yep. Tried to fit me up with an assault charge but

couldn't make it stick. My brief picked so many holes in his evidence it looked like a piece of Edam.' He fidgeted with his gold chain. 'Imagine it… me? It's ridiculous. I wouldn't dream of doing anyone harm. My dear old mother brought me up to be kind to people. Wouldn't want her fretting in her grave, would I?'

Shanahan spluttered into his glass. 'Sure, Mel. By the way, did you know the other stooge, Colin Mason?'

'Never heard of him. You?'

'He worked here a while back, on the door. Had to let him go; only turned up for work when it suited. Had a problem with alcohol after his wife left him. By the way, how well do you know Hazel Mackie?'

'Steve never involved her,' said Toomey, 'he was two-timing her.'

'That's a bit rich coming from you, Mel. Who was it?'

'I never got a name. I heard him on the blower one day when I was in his office. When I asked who it was, he gave me a story about it being one of his clients. How many clients do you call "darling", I ask you?'

'And if Hazel found out about it?' asked Shanahan.

'She might just be angry enough to want him dead,' said Toomey, putting down his empty glass with a clunk. 'If you hear any more from Crawford, let me know, will you?'

'He was asking after you. Only a matter of time before he comes knocking,' said Shanahan.

'Let him come, if he's got the guts. Last time he came calling, it didn't end well for him.'

# DAY TEN

Wednesday, 6 April 1983

# THIRTY-TWO

Beeston, 11am: Kate was going over what Matt had told her about the accident in her head as she approached Ellie Price's place in a heavy shower of rain. It was the smartest in the row of terraced houses on Imperial Road, with a bay window and a newly painted black front door with brass knocker. She tapped three times, stepped back and waited. Someone passed behind her on the street. She turned to see a tall man walking in the direction of the newsagents on the corner, splashing through puddles in his heavy boots. The collar of his greatcoat was pulled up, shielding his face, but she noticed his bristly ginger hair. He stopped after a few paces, leant up against a wall and lit a cigarette, shielding it from the rain with his hand. He glanced back in her direction before moving off. As she was watching to see where he'd go, she heard the click of the door opening. She turned back to see an anxious-looking, silky-haired woman peering around it. Her face softened when she set eyes on Kate.

'Mrs Brooks, do come in. I'm afraid you'll have to take me as you find me today. I have just got back from shopping.'

Ellie led her to a front parlour room with a red stone fireplace, a hearth rug, a sideboard, two easy chairs and the smell of furniture polish. There was little else aside from a large silver crucifix on the sideboard and a framed poster on the chimney breast which read "IN GOD WE TRUST". She ushered Kate to a chair facing the front window and offered her a drink. Kate asked for a glass of water, and while she waited for Ellie to bring it, two women in raincoats hurried past outside, armed with umbrellas. A few moments later, Ellie returned with her drink, then sat on the edge of the other chair, arms folded, smiling nervously.

Although Matt had said that Ellie would find Kate far less intimidating than him, her experience as a journalist made her aware of the need to create a relaxed setting and choose the right moments to force the issue.

Kate leaned back in the chair casually, her hands resting on her lap. 'Are you okay with answering a few routine questions?' she asked in a nonchalant tone, taking a sip from her glass.

Ellie blew out her cheeks, breathing out with a puff. 'I'll do my best.'

'You've heard the sad news of Steve Mackie?'

Ellie gave her a solemn nod. 'Yes, I have. May God rest his soul.'

'I understand you and Steve were quite close.'

'For a time, yes we were,' said Ellie with a shallow sigh.

'You were sharing grief over Carl's death, is that so?'

'I suppose so, yes.'

'And you were kind enough to lend him money, something you later regretted?'

Ellie pinched the bridge of her nose. 'He seemed to be just like me – broken. I wanted to help.'

'Could you say why you came to regret helping Steve?'

'I can't,' said Ellie, with rising colour in her olive cheeks.

'Let me make things easier for you,' said Kate, fixing her in the eye. 'We know about your affair. Hazel told us that when she found out about it, she had to tell you the truth about the accident. She said you promised her you would keep silent. But it doesn't matter now, does it? Now that Steve's dead?'

'I'm very ashamed of what I did,' said Ellie, staring into space. 'The flesh is weak.'

'You must have been angry too. When you found out that Steve had driven Carl to his death and covered it up?'

Ellie's eyes began to bulge. 'What are you suggesting? That I might have... that's ridiculous. I called Steve because I wanted to talk. What he did was sinful, but I do forgive him. Nothing I could ever do would bring Carl back. I have to live with the regret that my last words to my one and only son were said in anger.'

'You argued?'

'On the night of his stag party. I was against his marriage; his fiancée refused to take our religion. They were to be married in a registry office, without God's blessing. I wish I could turn back time, take back everything I said and just tell him how much I loved him.'

'What about Carl's father? Does he know the truth?'

'Yes, he does.' She paused for a few seconds. 'I know I promised Hazel, but I had to tell Carl's father that his son was innocent.'

'How did he react?'

'He was shocked, angry. He wanted me to go to the police, but I told him why I couldn't, that it was pointless; Steve could deny it all anyway. Reluctantly, he agreed.'

'You are separated, divorced?' asked Kate.

Ellie swallowed hard. 'We split up before Carl was born. He couldn't marry me, and he made me swear never to tell a soul who he was.'

'And you intend to keep that promise?'

Ellie's look was solemn. 'Yes I do. That's the one secret I *will* take to my grave.'

Raindrops were trickling down her forehead as Kate walked uphill in the direction of her parked Mini. As she tried to squint the water out of her eyes, she narrowly avoided a collision with a man coming the other way. Kate was distracted by thoughts about Ellie Price. It was hard to reconcile the deeply religious doting mother with the woman who'd had a fling with her son's married friend. It sounded as if it wasn't her first affair either. But was Ellie capable of violence, of killing someone? She wanted to say no, but then Ellie had been lied to and cheated by the man who'd killed her own flesh and blood. "The flesh is weak" Ellie had said. Those words were planted in Kate's head. She took a right turn at the next corner and her car came into sight. When she reached it, she unzipped her dripping handbag and found the car keys. As she put them into the lock, she could hear footsteps sploshing behind her. When she turned the key, they stopped. A face, blurred by the rainfall, appeared above her own reflection in the car window. A strong hand pressed against her lips, stifling her scream. The next thing she felt was a dull, painful thud at the back of her skull and, in a single heartbeat, dark curtains closed across her eyes.

# THIRTY-THREE

West Bridgford, 1pm: Harry was staring through the lounge window into his garden. He'd asked Linda to leave them, and she had, somewhat reluctantly, retreated to the kitchen ten minutes earlier. He continued to avoid eye contact with Matt as he spoke, his voice strangled and weak. 'It seems you know the truth about the accident?'

Matt nodded. 'Yes, I do. But I still don't understand—'

'Who told you? Was it Hazel?' Harry turned his head to look Matt in the eye now.

'It doesn't matter how I found out,' said Matt, slipping out his notebook. 'What I need to know is what really happened that night.'

'Can you keep your voice down? Linda might hear us.'

Matt did a double take. 'You mean your wife doesn't know?'

'I promised Steve I'd tell nobody. I believe in keeping my word. But now he's... gone.' Harry's eyes started to well up.

'Must be hard for you.'

'Yes, I still can't quite believe he was murdered.'

'How is Linda taking it? I understand she and Steve were close.'

Harry gave him a quizzical look. 'I'm not sure what you mean by that.'

'Eddie Fletcher told us they regularly met at the rowing club for drinks. You must have known that, surely?'

Harry's face reddened. 'Y... yes, of course I did. So what? We were like a family. You can't be suggesting... Steve and Linda... that's absurd.'

Matt leant in closer to Harry to eyeball him. 'What I do know is that if you found out that the man you lied for was having an affair with your wife, you would be understandably outraged.'

Harry huffed. 'You think I killed Steve? Now you're in fantasy land.'

'If you say so. But I would like you to explain one more thing to me. Why were you protecting him?'

'I was protecting myself too,' said Harry rubbing his flimsy, wasted legs. When he stopped, Matt saw that his hands were trembling.

'Take your time,' said Matt, softening his tone. 'Tell me exactly how it happened.'

Harry coughed, then cleared his throat. 'That night, Carl picked me up first, then Steve. He drove us into town, and we parked up on Castle Boulevard. His plan was to share a taxi home and then come back for the car in the morning. We were having a good time in the Cross Keys, but it all started to go sour when Carl decided to give his mum a call. I've already told you about the argument he had and the scuffle with Steve. We were asked to leave, so we made our way down to the Flying Horse. We couldn't keep pace with Carl after that and he refused to stop drinking, until he fell over, that was.'

'Was he hurt?'

'Not that I could tell; he wouldn't have felt anything. He'd been gone a long while to the gents, so I went looking. Found him on the floor, head propped up against a wall with a silly grin on his face. I got Steve to come and help me pick him up. The only way he could walk was between us, with his arms around our shoulders. When we got to the taxi rank, there was a massive queue. It wasn't far to the car, so Steve's plan was to get him there and drive his car back. I was too far gone to realise what a dumb idea it was. When we reached the car, Steve took the car keys from Carl's pocket. We helped him onto the back seat and left him slumped across it. The first stop was to be Carl's house in Bramcote village. We never got there.'

'How did it happen?'

'We'd turned off the dual carriageway onto an unlit country lane. It was close to midnight, and it was quiet. Steve was driving too fast; he was joking about Carl not being able to take his drink. Something… I'll never know… a cat, a fox maybe, appeared in our headlight beam. Steve swerved, lost control. We careered across the verge and into a massive tree. My side of the car was crushed, and Carl was thrown against a rear door. He had no chance. I heard Steve get out of the car and get into the back. I tried to move but realised I was trapped. The next thing I saw was Steve pushing Carl into the driver's seat.'

Matt looked up from his notetaking. 'How did he do that?'

'Steve is… was a rower, very strong. I saw him recline the driver's seat then manhandle Carl over it, legs first. Then he raised the seat again, went to the front and placed Carl's head on the steering wheel. I think he thought I was dead too, because when he looked across to me and saw my eyes open, he let out a gasp.'

'What did he say to you?'

'That he'd get help, but first we had to get our story straight. There was nothing we could do to save Carl now. But if the police knew that Steve was the driver, he would be facing prison. He told me that I was responsible too. We had both put Carl on the back seat, unbelted. When I look back, I know I shouldn't have gone along with it. I shouldn't have let the world think that Carl was the drunken driver, that he crippled me. But I didn't want my wife and daughter to know what I'd done, nor did I want Steve to go to gaol. After all, it was just a stupid, stupid accident.' Harry paused to run his fingers through his unkempt, thick mop of hair. 'You should know that you are the first person I've ever talked to about this.'

'I know this isn't easy for you.'

'I wouldn't blame you for thinking me a pathetic fool.'

'I don't as a matter of fact. I do, however, see that Steve Mackie was a master manipulator.'

There was a prolonged silence, broken by Harry's croaky voice. 'What should I do next?' he asked, swallowing hard.

'Look at this as a chance to redeem yourself. I suggest that you speak to Linda and Zoe when I leave. You may find that they are more understanding than you had imagined.'

'And then?'

'The police will need to be informed. I could do this for you, but I think it would be better if you went voluntarily and made a statement. I can recommend a good lawyer if you like. And when you've done that, maybe you'll want to make your apologies to Mrs Price?'

Harry's mouth dropped open. 'Ellie knows?'

'Yes. Hazel told her when she found out she was having an affair with Steve.'

# THIRTY-FOUR

On his way through the front door, Matt picked up some post from the doormat. He reached the office door and was surprised to find it locked. There was no answer when he rang the bell, so he took his keys from his pocket and let himself in, wondering at the same time where Kate could have got to. Desmond was dozing on her chair. As he approached, the cat stretched out a paw and yawned. Matt threw the post onto Kate's desk, but one letter slid onto the floor. He picked it up and saw it was addressed to him and unstamped. Matt tore it open and unfolded a single sheet of paper. Letters cut from newspaper headlines were pasted onto it. They formed a simple, stark message: "BACK OFF OR NEXT TIME SHE IS DEAD".

Matt hurried through to his office, pulled open a drawer and flicked through some index cards before finding Ellie Price's details. He picked up the phone receiver and punched the numbers in.

'Mrs Price? It's Matt Crawford.'

'Mr Crawford. Is there something I can help with?'

'I hope so. Was Kate with you this morning?'

'Yes, she was.'

'When did she leave?'

'Let me think… it was before midday. I know that because I was at the church by 12pm.' Then, after a moment's silence, 'Is something wrong?'

'No, it's nothing; I just needed a word. She's probably caught up in traffic.'

Matt put down the receiver and immediately dialled again. There was no answer from Kate's home number; he decided to go there. As he was picking up his car keys from the desk, the phone rang. The woman's voice was hard to decipher; there was a clamour in the background.

'Am I speaking to Mr Crawford?'

'Yes, but I can't hear you very well. Who's calling?'

She raised her voice. 'This is the Queen's Medical Centre. We have a patient here in casualty who asked us to call you, a Mrs Kate Brooks… Mr Crawford… can you hear me?'

Matt's heart was racing; he had taken the receiver away from his mouth to get his breath back. 'Sorry… yes. What's happened to her? Is she okay?'

'Please don't be alarmed. She's had an accident, but she is sitting up and talking. A doctor has examined her, and we will be moving her onto a ward shortly.'

He caught his breath. 'Tell Kate I'm on my way.'

The smell of disinfectant made him feel nauseous; for a horrible moment he was time travelling back to the long days he'd spent in a hospital bed after his stabbing.

Matt stopped in front of the door to the ward and took a deep breath. He thrust his shoulders back and pushed the door open. He checked in at the reception desk, where a nurse gave him directions. He weaved his way past trolleys and nursing staff until he found himself at her bedside. Her auburn hair had a wide bandage wrapped around it. She looked very pale and drowsy-eyed but did manage to raise a weak smile when she saw him. He pulled up a chair and sat close to her so that he could speak softly.

'Got here as soon as I could. How are you?'

'As you see, I'm fine. It's just a little bump on the head. Told them I wanted to go home, but they won't let me. They want to do an X-ray and then see how I am overnight.'

'What happened?'

'I must have been hit from behind as I was getting into my car. When I came round, I was being tossed around in the back of an ambulance and a strange man was asking me my name. I don't like it here; it's noisy and the bed's too hard. Can you take me home?'

'I'm afraid you'll have to stay put until the doctor gives you the all-clear.'

'But—'

'No ifs or buts, Kate. You're probably concussed.'

She frowned. 'But all they're giving me is painkillers. I can take them at home.'

'They have to check for complications. Where were you when it happened?'

'Close to Ellie Price's place, where I'd par...' She was suddenly distracted by something she saw over his shoulder. Matt turned to see a blond-haired man with a chiselled chin and a deep tan. 'Luke... I... I said not to come.'

Luke moved closer and stood at the end of the bed. 'I had to see you.'

Kate frowned. 'Very thoughtful I'm sure, but—'

'I suppose this is your boss?' asked Luke, nodding towards Matt.

Matt rose from his chair, stepped forwards and shook hands. 'Matt Crawford.'

'The famous detective no less,' he said with a sarcastic grin. 'Shame we couldn't meet in better circumstances.' Luke released his hand and nodded towards Kate. 'I warned her this was a risky business.'

'You think I didn't?' said Matt, beginning to bristle.

While Luke was taking off his coat, Kate caught Matt's attention. She slowly shook her head and mouthed "not now". Matt reluctantly accepted this was not the right moment. What he wanted to tell Luke was that Kate was her own person, that she did not dance to his tune or anyone else's. That she was as clever as she was brave. Instead, he politely made his excuses and slipped out of the room, promising Kate he'd look in on her again tomorrow.

\*\*\*

Back in his flat, Matt lay back on the sofa listening to a John Lennon album and thought about Kate, lying in her hospital bed. He had failed her. The warning signs had been there; he'd felt eyes on him outside Shanahan's club and again that night with Fiona. He should never have let Kate go to Ellie Price's alone. When he was growing up, his policeman dad had told him many times what it meant to be a man. A real man stands up for the truth; a real man admits when he's wrong. But most of all he moves heaven and earth to protect his loved ones from harm. After today, he knew one thing for sure. He was never ever going to let this happen again.

He was on his way to the fridge for a can of beer when the phone rang in the hall. He'd hoped it might be Kate, but his heart sank when he heard Fiona's voice. He did his best to affect a chirpy tone.

'You must be telepathic. I was just thinking about you,' he said, trying to sound convincing.

'Really, darling? I'm glad to hear it. I'm having a dinner party at my place on Friday night, just a few friends. Was wondering if you'd like to come?'

'I'd love to, but I'm afraid I can't. Kate's in hospital; she's been attacked.'

'She's what? Is she okay?'

'She has concussion. They've got her under observation.'

'That's awful; when did this happen?'

'This morning, as she was getting into her car.'

'Where was she?'

'In Beeston, visiting someone.'

'Did the attacker steal anything?'

'No, they weren't after money.'

'Then, what was it about?' she asked, with concern in her voice.

'Someone doesn't like us poking our nose into the murders.'

Matt heard her gasp. 'Bloody hell, Matt, you are having a bad time. First the news about Amanda and now this happens to Kate.'

'I'm sorry? What about Amanda?'

'Haven't you heard? She and her accountant have announced their engagement.'

He couldn't find any words for a moment.

'Matt, are you still there?'

'Yes… sorry. Look, I'd better go. Sorry I can't make it for dinner. I'll call you when things are better.'

Matt put down the receiver and walked back into the kitchen. John Lennon's distinctive, isolated voice wafted through from the lounge; he was singing "Jealous Guy".

# DAY ELEVEN

Thursday, 7 April 1983

# THIRTY-FIVE

The Crawford Agency, 8.30am: 'You think that the attack on Kate is connected to the murders?' asked DI Martin, stroking his eyebrows; their grey sprouts gave him the look of a wizard. Prompted by the attack on Kate, Joe Martin had been an unexpected early arrival. Matt had been chewing on a piece of toast in his flat. He'd come to the front door in his slippers and shown the inspector through to his office.

'I'm sure there's a link,' said Matt, 'and I'll show you why.' He opened a drawer, pulled out an envelope and slid it across his desk to the policeman.

DI Martin took out a pair of glasses from his inside pocket, opened the envelope and unfolded the note. When he'd finished reading, he bit hard on his lip. 'Next time she is dead. You think the "she" is Kate?'

'Who else could it be?' said Matt with a sarcastic grin.

'When did you get this?'

'It came by hand yesterday.'

The DI put the message back into the envelope and pocketed it. 'You should have come to us earlier. Any idea who might have sent it?'

'Only a hunch. We've been rattling Michael Shanahan's cage. Know him? He and Steve Mackie were poker buddies.'

The DI smiled. 'Yes, he's a person of interest.'

'You know that Steve Mackie owed him money big time?'

DI Martin gave a wry smile. 'Him and quite a few others, it seems.'

'Including my old pal, Mel Toomey.'

'Yes, we know about him too as it happens.'

'Has the coroner reported yet?' asked Matt.

The DI hesitated. 'I shouldn't really be sharing this with you.'

'But?'

'I suppose you'll hear it from Hazel soon enough. It confirms that Steve Mackie died from gunshot wounds, bullets fired from a revolver entering through his back. He has bruises to his arms and torso and rope burns on his wrists.'

'Time of death?'

'Between 7pm and 10pm the day he went missing.'

Matt paused for thought. 'The same time frame as Colin Mason by any chance?'

'Your assumption is correct.'

'Have you searched the house in Beeston yet? Where the taxi dropped Steve.'

'Forensics are there now.'

'When I was there with Steve's secretary, I saw a length of rope in the garden. Could have—'

'Been used to tie his hands with. Thanks, I'll check it out.' DI Martin took out a notebook and jotted down the details.

'There is one more thing I should mention about our visit to the house,' said Matt.

The inspector's pen was poised. 'I'm listening.'

'We disturbed an intruder. He'd been dossing down there.'

'Get a good look at the guy?'

'Afraid not, couldn't keep up with him; not as fit as I used to be.'

The DI's eyes moved to Matt's chest. 'With good reason.'

'But the next-door neighbour got a closer glimpse. He's tall with dark hair, wearing jeans and a checked shirt. Problem is, she didn't see his face.'

The DI coughed. 'Not much to go on, but I'll make a note. What's her name?'

'Mrs Tindall. She's the one who spotted the blue transit van parked outside.'

'Yes, we're looking into that.'

'What did the coroner say about the other victim?'

'This is not for public release, you understand. Colin Mason died from a single blow to the head from a large, heavy object.'

'You think we're looking at the same killer?'

'Too early to say; we haven't recovered any murder weapons. After what you've just shown me, I'm going to have your building watched along with your assistant's apartment. I'll be having a word with Mrs Brooks later.'

'Please go easy, Joe, she's a bit fragile.'

'Don't worry, son, I'll handle her with care. By the way, why was she visiting Mrs Price?'

'Steve and Ellie Price were having an affair; he owed money to her too.'

The DI smiled ruefully. 'Now that we didn't know.'

*There's plenty more you don't know*, thought Matt, *but for now I want to stay one step ahead.*

After showing the DI to the door, Matt returned to Kate's desk to open the post. The first letter he opened was from a solicitor representing the canoodling councillor's wife. He was inviting Matt to a meeting at their offices so that they could prepare the court case and examine the photographic evidence, which he appeared well pleased with. Matt binned a couple of flyers from local restaurants before opening the next letter. It was a cheque from Hazel Mackie in full payment of his last invoice; Kate would be happy now that they could pay off their rent arrears. He remembered that it was Kate who talked him into taking the case. But money was of secondary importance right now; he needed to ensure her safety.

He put the solicitor's appointment in the diary on Kate's desk before returning to his own office to phone the hospital. The ward sister informed him that Kate had been discharged earlier. He put the receiver down and called her flat.

'The hospital told me you'd been allowed home. How are you?'

'I'm absolutely fine; I'll be with you shortly. Luke is going to drop me off.'

His heart dipped at the sound of that name. 'I have another suggestion. I'll come over to you. Please ask Luke to stay with you until I arrive.'

She gave a sigh. 'I know that you are concerned about me, but there's no reason for me to stay off work.'

'I'll explain when I get there. See you in twenty minutes.'

***

They were sitting at Kate's kitchen table drinking tea; Matt's was now lukewarm and undrinkable. Kate was fidgeting with the dressing which interrupted the auburn curls at the back of her head. A few minutes before, Matt had watched Luke kiss her pale cheek as he left the flat. Luke hadn't said a single word to him, unless you counted the grunt when Matt had arrived. Probably for the best, as Matt was already struggling to suppress an urge to punch his nose. After Luke had left, Matt told Kate about the visit from DI Martin and the threatening note. Then he gave her an instruction to stay at home and lie low for a while until the wound healed.

She sat with her arms crossed. 'I can't believe you're siding with Luke. You think I'm not up to this job.'

'Kate, you've just been attacked; I'm suggesting you take a break to recover. The police will be keeping a watch on you here. It will be much safer for you.'

Colour rushed to her cheeks. 'If I'd wanted safe, I'd have stayed working on the paper. I'm not going to walk away just because some crank thinks they can manipulate us. This is ridiculous. We are in the middle of the biggest case we've ever had and you're telling me I should take a holiday? And what about our clients? We both know that you can't run the agency single-handed. I even have to remind you to feed the cat.'

He knew she was right; they had built up the agency together. Without her, he would be overstretched and disorganised. Reluctantly, he relented, agreeing that she would be back at the agency in the morning to update him on Ellie Price. But there was something he needed to ask before he left.

'Your attacker. Did you get a close look?'

'I only saw a blurred reflection in the car window. But I did notice someone while I was waiting outside Ellie's earlier. He was tall, well over six foot, with spikey ginger hair, wearing a black greatcoat. The collar was pulled up so I couldn't see much of his face. But I did notice his boots, shiny Doc Martins.'

# DAY TWELVE

Friday, 8 April 1983

# THIRTY-SIX

8.30am: on her way from the car park to the front door, Kate nodded a "good morning" to the suited man in a doorway, who was trying just a little too hard to mingle with the ordinary world of office staff on their way to work. His upright stance and darting eyes told her he must be plain-clothes police. Kate made her way along the corridor and unlocked the office door. She put her bag down on her desk and hung her coat up on the peg, then headed for the kitchen. The sink was filled with unwashed mugs and bowls smeared with cat food. Teaspoons had been left dripping on the work surface. Kate flicked the kettle on and, while it boiled, she filled the sink with hot water and Fairy Liquid. *What possessed that man to think he could manage without me? Two days and it smells like rats' breath in here.*

Back at her desk, she took two aspirin tablets from a bottle in her bag and washed them down with a mouthful of tea. A late night at the station with DI Martin reliving the attack on her had taken its toll, but Kate was not going to let her throbbing head hold her back. As she was sorting through the post strewn across her desk, the door clicked open and Matt came in, the cat in his arms.

'Look, Desmond, Auntie Kate is back,' he said, pointing towards her.

Her face broke into a weak smile. 'And not a moment too soon by the look of it.'

He put the cat onto the leather sofa and cleared his throat. 'I am er… sorry about the state of the office.'

'Apology accepted. Let me get you a coffee and I'll tell you about my chat with Ellie Price.'

Matt gave her his full attention as she shared her thoughts about the contradictions she had found in Ellie. A deeply religious woman who flirted with married men. A devoted mother who argued fiercely over religion with her son. A young lady who had made a solemn promise to a man who had walked away from their child. Ellie must have gone ballistic when she discovered Steve's part in her son's fatal crash. Had that driven her to a revenge killing? It was possible, but Kate had her doubts.

'Good work,' said Matt. 'With what you've told me, she's got to stay on our radar. So has Harry Barton. Although he denies it, I'm wondering if he found out Steve and his wife Linda were seeing one another.'

'And then killed him… you think he would go that far?' asked Kate.

'Obviously not without assistance; he could have hired someone to do it for him.'

'That would cost. Does he have that sort of money?'

'I'm not sure. I've been wondering about your attacker; I think I might know him,' said Matt, narrowing his eyes.

Kate felt her neck tighten as she waited for him to continue. 'Are you going to tell me his name?'

'Your description fits that of a guy I met at the Montague club. His name's Gerry; he works on the door.'

'Know much about him?'

'No, but I rang the club last night and found out his surname is Dunne. I've asked my brother Richard to check on—' The ring of the phone interrupted him; Kate picked it up. 'Crawford Detective Agency. How can I help?'

The deep, gritty voice on the other end was familiar. 'Hello, Mrs Brooks, it's DI Martin here. Can I speak to Matt?'

'Certainly, Inspector, I'll pass you over.' She handed the receiver to Matt who had got to his feet and stood by her desk, close enough for her to listen in.

'What have you got for me, Joe?' asked Matt.

The inspector's tone was unusually upbeat. 'The van you tipped us off about, I think we've found it.'

'Where?' asked Matt.

'In Sawley, the landlord at The Navigation reported an abandoned van in the car park.'

Matt paused for a couple of seconds. 'That would figure. It's about three miles from the murder scene.'

'The vehicle fits the description you gave me: a blue Ford Transit.'

'Did you check the back lights? If you recall, the neighbour said one of them was knocked out.'

There was a crackle on the line. 'Yes, one of them is smashed and there's crash damage to the front.'

'Have you traced the owner?'

'It's registered to a builder in Bramcote, but he claims it's not his. He said someone nicked the number plates from his transit three weeks ago, so he bought a new set.'

'I hope you gave him a ticking off for not reporting it.'

'My DS gave him an earful.'

Kate watched Matt roll his eyes as he thanked the inspector and put the phone down. 'Seems pleased with himself,' she remarked.

'It's a nice break. Maybe it'll get the men upstairs off his back for a couple of days.'

'When are you going to tell him about Gerry Dunne?'

'Only when I'm certain Gerry's our man. Let's see what my brother comes up with. In the meantime, maybe you could get back to finding out about that barmaid at Shanahan's. Please tread very carefully; only talk to people you trust, and don't tell them why we're interested.'

'Okay, I'll ask around,' she said, wondering how much Matt's preoccupation with this woman was prejudicing the direction of their investigation. Then there was his attraction to Hazel.

'Meant to ask,' she said, 'did you get hold of the loan sharks?'

'Yes, did a deal. I said I wouldn't report them for harassment if they let Hazel pay them back interest free.'

'Good news.'

Matt sighed. 'Trouble is, it's just the tip of the iceberg.' He glanced down at his watch. 'Sorry, I have to make tracks now. Meeting up with an old friend from my former life. Jack's just the man we need to help sniff out a villain. He's been a bit down on his luck recently, so he'll be grateful for some cash in hand.'

'Just because Hazel Mackie's cheque has arrived, there's no need to go splashing it around too soon. Our divorce work has gone a bit quiet lately.'

His grin was sardonic. 'Perhaps monogamy is back in fashion.'

She frowned. 'I somehow doubt that.'

Kate was aware of his grey-blue eyes locking onto hers. 'I'm sorry, I didn't mean to make light of people's marriage problems. How are things with Luke?'

She wasn't sure how to react. They didn't ever talk about each other's personal lives. There had been one exception last winter. They'd gone out for drinks to celebrate successfully reuniting an elderly woman with her long-lost sister. After their client had left and she'd had more wine, Kate had given Matt an embarrassingly tearful account of the day she discovered Luke in bed with Glennis, "the tennis club floozy". Matt had listened to her outpourings, and he'd put his arm around her shoulder as they walked back from the pub. She felt respected, recognised and, dare she think it, loved.

Kate found herself stammering. 'He... he... says he's worried about me. I told him I'm not his responsibility anymore.'

'What did he say to that?' asked Matt.

She hesitated, not wanting to tell him. 'He said he still loves me; he wants me back.'

'And you?'

Her head felt fuzzy, and her ears were filled with a high-pitched ringing. 'I don't know anymore; I really don't know.'

# THIRTY-SEVEN

The café smelled of bacon and fried bread; he and Jack were waiting for their full English breakfast to arrive. A young girl wiped the melamine tabletop with a wet cloth and put the sauce bottles and condiments back on their table. Matt's eyes danced around the room. In the far corner, two workmen in oil-stained blue overalls sat smoking roll-ups while analysing the last Forest game. On the next table, a middle-aged man was studying the headlines of the *Daily Express* over a steaming mug of tea. Thieves had stolen £7 million in cash from a Security Express van in London. *Most likely an inside job.*

Outside, grey clouds hung heavy over city shoppers as they walked along pavements still damp from yesterday's rain. Sitting here with his old friend, it was almost as if time had reversed, and he was back on the force. Jack Greaves, an ex-con, had been one of his most valued and reliable informers. Six months back, Matt heard that Jack had been sidelined by the new DI in the Drugs Squad. Matt knew Jack needed the money to pay for his ageing mother's care.

'What you got for me?' asked Jack, pulling at grey strands of hair at the tip of his goatee.

Matt lowered his voice. 'Mel Toomey. Know him, Greavesie?'

'You know I do.'

'I need some information on him. Nobody needs to know who is asking. I know I can trust you, and I'll make it worth your while.' Matt pulled a roll of ten-pound notes from his pocket, peeled five off and slid them across the table. 'This is for starters.'

Jack picked up the notes, counted them and tucked them into the top pocket of his worn corduroy jacket. 'What is it you...'

The waitress appeared over Jack's shoulder and put two heaped plates in front of them. Jack picked up a sausage with his fingers and took a healthy bite. He was still chewing as he continued. 'Not bad here, is it? What you want to know about two-timing Toomey?'

Matt chuckled. 'Hadn't heard that one before; sounds about right. Give me the usual run-down on him. How he's making his money, where he drinks, who he's shacked up with, who his friends are. Look out for any mention of his mate Shady Shanahan or Steve Mackie; they are, or were, poker buddies.'

Jack, who had a fork load of bacon poised near his mouth, let it drop back onto his plate. 'The guy who was shot... you think Toomey was involved in that?'

'He's definitely on my shortlist. By the way, I need this yesterday.'

***

The first thing he noticed when he got back was that Kate had more colour in her face. 'You smell like a transport café,' she said, pinching her nostrils.

'Jack likes a fry-up.'

She gave him her school mistress frown. 'And you don't of course… who is he exactly?'

'Information is his stock-in-trade.'

'A snitch?'

He nodded. 'One of the best.'

'How did it go?'

'He's going to see what he can dig up on Toomey.'

'Good news then. I've got some too.' She looked down at her notepad before continuing. 'I've been phoning around some of my friends. One of them, Jasmine, I know from the squash club. She's also a regular at the Dancing Magpie. When I described the barmaid, she told me she's called Tamara. Apparently, she's been there for about a year. Jasmine knows a guy who used to go out with Tamara, so she's going to ask him about her.'

'That's brilliant, Kate. And she realises the delicacy?'

'Our names will not be mentioned.'

'Good. Anything else happen while I was out?'

Her cheeky grin was back. 'Yes. I fed your cat and… oh… there was one more thing. Your brother called and wants you to ring back.'

Matt made a beeline for his office and dialled Richard's

236

number.

'Kate said you wanted a word?'

'That's right. I've got something on your man Gerry Dunne.'

'Thought you might have. What's he been up to?'

'He was charged with assault in November 1981. He floored a young guy in Yates Wine Lodge. But two weeks later the victim, a student, retracted his statement and charges were dropped.'

'Someone got to him?'

'Could be. Anyway, your Mr Dunne has been in trouble before. Back in 1972, he was jailed for two years for a violent attack on a police officer in West Belfast. The officer's face was so badly disfigured he had to have plastic surgery. His file says that Dunne's father was killed by an RUC officer during sectarian violence in Londonderry in 1969. Gerry would have been seventeen years old. He and his younger sister came over to Nottingham in 1975 to start a new life, leaving his older sister and mother back in Belfast.'

'An angry young man.'

'Looks that way,' said Richard. 'Are you going to tell me why you're interested in him?'

'He could be the guy who attacked Kate.'

'What makes you think that?'

'I've met Mr Dunne; he works on the door at the Montague club. He's a perfect fit for Kate's description and after what you just told me—'

'Have you shared this with DI Martin?'

'Not yet. I wanted to be sure.'

There was silence on the line for a few seconds. 'I hope this is not all about you wanting to prove yourself. For what it's worth, we already know you are a great detective. Now, promise me you're going to update Joe Martin, or I'll have to do it myself.'

'Okay, I promise. Know where I can find him right now?'

'He's here at the station. He's pulled Michael Shanahan in for questioning.'

'About bloody time.'

Matt thanked his brother, then put the receiver down. He took a sketch pad from his desk drawer along with an artist's pencil and a rubber. Then, he closed his eyes for a moment, opened them again, picked up the pencil and started to draw.

# THIRTY-EIGHT

Central Police Station, 1pm: Michael Shanahan blinked. The strip lighting in the interview room was irritating his eyes. He pulled his sunglasses from the top pocket of his jacket and placed them carefully on the bridge of his nose. *Now they can't read my eyes; it's just like a four player poker table. Two police, my brief and me.*

The older police officer, DI Martin, shuffled in his chair before opening the proceedings. 'Mr Shanahan, you do know why you're here?'

'Something to do with the estate agent, I suppose. The one who was murdered.'

DI Martin smiled. 'Right in one. Steve Mackie is his name, as you well know. You both belonged to the Montague club and played poker together. Is that right?'

He glanced over at his solicitor before confirming. 'Yep, we did.'

'Seems he owed you a large sum of money. How much exactly?'

'Three grand,' he replied, and as he did so, he saw the younger officer, DS Crowther, make a note on his pad.

'How long ago did he lose this money to you?' asked the DI.

Shanahan stroked his sideburn. 'Can't say exactly. Maybe three months.'

'Did you, or any of your minions, try to collect?'

'I phoned him a few times, but it was always mañana with Steve.'

'So, you decided to use force to get your money, is that right?' said DI Martin, fixing him in the eye.

Shanahan's solicitor, silent until now, intervened. 'Inspector, I don't know where this is leading, but my client is not a violent man.'

'Then maybe your client can tell us where he was on the evening of 23 March.'

Shanahan sneered. 'I was at my club as usual, the whole evening and into the night. There are several of my staff who can vouch for that.'

'Fine, we'll need their names. Give them to DS Crowther when we are finished here.'

'And you expect us to believe that you were just going to sit back and let Steve Mackie off the hook?' asked DS Crowther, looking up from his notes. 'Assuming you were at your club as you say, who did you pay to take care of Mr Mackie that night?'

Shanahan's face reddened with anger, but his solicitor put his hand up to stop his client talking. 'My client will not dignify this ridiculous question with a response. Now if there are no further questions?'

'I have one more as it happens,' said DI Martin. 'The other victim, Colin Mason, how well did you know him, Mr Shanahan?'

'Hardly at all.'

'Really? I'm surprised. Our records show he worked on the door of your nightclub for nine months. He left just over a year ago. Can you tell me why?'

Shanahan scratched his ear. 'Come to think of it, I do remember something now. Bruce said he couldn't rely on him, so we gave him the push. Liked the bottle too much.'

The solicitor cleared his throat. 'Now if that's all.'

'That's it, for now at least,' said DI Martin, getting up from his chair. 'If you'll just leave those names with my DS, I'll bid you both good day, until next time.'

\*\*\*

Beeston Marina, 3pm: the only outside guests at the Marina Café were an elderly man with a notched walking stick and his bull terrier. Matt nodded a "good afternoon" as he walked by on his way to the front door, which was wedged open. As he got closer, the hum of conversation reached him and so did the smell of cigarette smoke and burnt toast. The lady he'd first met on the fateful day he discovered Steve's tie hurried past him with a tray full of steaming drinks and hot buttered teacakes. He stood at the counter waiting for her to return, and when she did, there was a faint smile of recognition as she swept straggles of her blonde hair away from her eyes.

'You're that detective, aren't you? What do you want this time?'

'Coffee with milk.'

'Take a seat; I'll bring it over.'

He found a small table near the window from which he could see her spooning instant coffee into a mug before filling it with boiling water from a large stainless steel heater and stirring in milk from a bottle. She bustled up to the table, and as she placed the drink on it, some coffee spilled over.

'Oops, I'll get a cloth.'

'No need for that. But there is something else you might help with.'

She stood upright, hands on hips. 'I knew this was coming. Look, if it's about the murders, I've told the police everything I know, which is not much. I've got a café to run in case you lot hadn't noticed.'

'This won't take a moment,' he said, slipping a folded sheet of paper from his inside pocket. He opened it out and handed it to her, thinking how grateful he was to his art teacher for noticing his keen eye and encouraging him to draw. 'The man in the sketch, do you recognise him?'

She held the picture at arm's length, tilted her head and squinted. 'His face is familiar, but I can't place… hold on, yes I remember now. A big guy with ginger hair. Looked a bit like a boxer.'

Matt felt his pulse quicken. 'Go on.'

'He was in here a few weeks back.'

'When exactly?'

She put her index finger to her bottom lip. 'As I recall, it was before the Easter holiday, and he was with a woman.'

'That would make it three weeks ago. The lady he was with, could you describe her?'

'She was one of them punk rockers, black T-shirt, leather jacket and spiked hair. They were talking to one of my regulars.'

'Did the boxer guy speak with an accent?'

'Yes, I did have trouble making him out. He was Irish.'

'Who were they speaking to?'

'His name's Dave. He's a homeless guy who hangs around here asking people for the price of a cup of tea. He's been down on his luck since he lost his job.'

'I need to talk to Dave. Any idea where I might find him?'

'I've seen him in the Boat and Horses of an evening. It's not far from here, on Trent Road.'

'What does he look like?'

'He's tall with dark hair down to his collar and a full beard. Looks about thirty, but I guess he's younger. Usually wears a faded denim jacket and patched-up jeans. There's a "ban the bomb" badge on the front of his jacket.'

Matt's excitement was growing. In his mind he was forming a picture of the figure that had run away from him at River Haven. It seemed like a good match. He thanked her and left a generous tip.

\*\*\*

Boat and Horses, 7pm: Thoughts were racing around his brain as he sat drinking his second pint of bitter, hoping for his target to appear. Friday night seemed like a good bet, but it was a full hour since opening time, and there was still no sign of anyone who looked remotely like Dave. Two men with ruddy, weathered faces sat at the bar discussing the pros and cons of the miners' strikes. A dog walker sat close by drinking Guinness, his panting whippet stretched out under a table. Another weekend stretched out in front of Matt, and he knew that most of it would be spent alone, if you discounted Desmond that was. No doubt Amanda and Guy would be making plans for the "big day". He wasn't sure about Kate. Maybe there would be a heart to heart with Luke? Matt wondered about Hazel. On the face of it, she was coping well. He could imagine her in a wine bar with friends. And what of Fiona? What would he say to her if she rang? And while all this was happening, there was a murderer out there who could strike again.

His neighbour woke the dog and trudged towards the door without finishing his drink. Before he got there, it opened slowly and a tall figure loped through it, letting the door close behind him and walking past the man and his dog as if they were invisible. He dragged his feet wearily in the direction of the bar, where he stood waiting to be served. Matt noticed his jeans had knee patches and he wore a checked lumberjack shirt. He couldn't be sure yet, but it was promising. The man ordered half a pint of shandy and counted out some coins before paying, then sauntered over to the table just vacated by the dog walker. The detective waited for him to settle in his chair before turning towards him and catching his eye.

'Dave, isn't it?' asked Matt.

The man sneered. 'Do I know you?'

'No, but we bumped into one another recently. Someone said I might find you here.'

'Who was that then?'

'Just someone down by the canal,' said Matt, making close eye contact. 'Look, I'm not going to mess you around. You were squatting in the empty house on Meadow Road. I was the one who chased after you when you ran off.'

Dave was taking short breaths now. 'Your place, is it? Cos, if it is, I ain't done nothing wrong. This guy said it was okay for me to kip down there for a while. He gave me the keys.'

'Which guy, what's his name?'

'I don't know. Met this Irish guy and his girlfriend in the Marina Café, and when I told them I had no place to go, they said they knew somewhere local. Said it belonged to a friend of theirs who was out of the country, and he wouldn't mind. Am I in any trouble?'

Matt leant over and put an arm on his shoulder. 'I'll level with you; it isn't my place. I'm a private detective working for the estate agent who's selling it. I'm not after you, I'm interested in the couple who gave you the keys. Can I get you something stronger than that shandy?'

Dave's eyes brightened. 'A whisky would warm me up.'

Two minutes later, Matt returned with a large scotch. He joined Dave at his table and saw his companion was looking a little more relaxed.

'This couple. Did they say anything else?' asked Matt.

'Not really. They bought me a cup of tea and a packet of cream custards. They're my favourite.'

'And you didn't catch their names?'

Dave took a good slug of whisky, then winced. 'Not his, but I heard him call her Tammy. I remember that because it made me think of Tammy Wynette… you know, the country singer.'

*Tammy, short for Tamara? The woman who stabbed me is Gerry Dunne's girlfriend.*

'When did you meet them? Can you give me a date?'

'Let me think… yes, it were a Thursday. It's a good day for me usually because the oldies have collected their pension from the post office and they're full of the joys.'

'Which Thursday would that be?'

Dave drained his glass and released a low purr of satisfaction. 'It were three weeks back, I'd say.'

'You sure?'

'Yes, the week before the Easter holidays. Kids were still at school.'

Matt tugged his diary from his jacket pocket and thumbed through the pages. 'So that would make it 24 March. Correct?'

*The day after Colin Mason and Steve Mackie were murdered.*

'Sounds about right,' replied Dave.

'Thanks, you've been very helpful. Just one last thing. I'll be needing those keys.'

Dave reached into his jeans pocket and placed them on the table next to his empty glass.

'That's good. Now, is there anything I might help you with?' asked Matt, noticing the keyring had a tag marked "RIVER HAVEN" as he picked it up.

Dave gave him a smile which exposed his tobacco-stained teeth. 'Well, there is one thing. I left me sleeping bag in the bedroom. Could you get it back for me? It gets cold at nights.'

'Can't promise anything I'm afraid. It's probably been taken away by the police as evidence.'

Dave's face reddened. 'The police have been there? Hold on a minute, you told me I wasn't in any trouble.'

'If what you've told me is the truth, you're not. For what it's worth, I believe you, and I'm sorry you don't have a roof over your head anymore.'

Matt got to his feet, pulled out his wallet, peeled away three ten-pound notes and slipped them into Dave's empty whisky glass. 'That should cover a sleeping bag and some new clothes. Take care.'

\*\*\*

Back at his flat, he fed Desmond and made himself a strong coffee before settling on the sofa in front of the TV to watch the news. A reporter had joined masses of protesters in Berkshire who were calling for nuclear disarmament. They had formed a chain fourteen miles long between three weapons centres. Then the programme cut to the next item: a murder investigation. Matt's eyes widened as he saw DI Joe Martin standing at a podium outside Nottingham Police HQ. Cameras were flashing into his face, and cameramen were pressing close to a barrier in front of him. He cleared his throat and adjusted the microphone before reading a prepared statement:

'We are investigating the murders of two Nottingham men, Colin Mason and Stephen Mackie. Both men were recently found in the vicinity of Beeston Weir on the river Trent. Firstly, I would like to thank those people who have already come forward with information; your co-operation is appreciated. We are currently following up on a number of leads and have interviewed one suspect, a local man in his forties, who has since been released. I am making a new appeal to anyone who might have been at Beeston Marina between the hours of 6pm and 11pm on Wednesday 23 March to come forward. If you saw or heard anything on that evening, please contact us.'

DI Martin spoke slowly and with authority; Matt was impressed. To his credit, the inspector remained unflustered when the press started firing questions at him:

'How were they killed exactly?'

'Who is the man you interviewed?'

'Were the two men friends?'

'Were they killed by the same person?'

'Is your investigation stalling?'

He told them politely he was not there to answer questions. Then he simply picked up his script, thanked them for coming, turned and walked briskly back to the station entrance, no doubt glad the TV ordeal was over.

# DAY THIRTEEN

Saturday, 9 April 1983

# THIRTY-NINE

It was lunchtime in Kate's flat. She and Jasmine were drinking Chablis and nibbling at egg mayonnaise sandwiches, cut into neat triangles of brown bread with no crusts. Kate had fleetingly thought about taking some of them down to the man on watch downstairs, but that might break his cover. What's more, she felt safe here in her lounge chatting to Jasmine; she was a good friend.

In the background, the radio was playing "Both Sides Now". Judy Collins was lamenting about how little we understand love. Kate wasn't sure whether she'd ever been in love with Luke and wondered why he wanted her back. Stranger than that, she didn't know why she was even considering the idea of giving him a second chance. She looked across to a vase filled with scented roses and freesias that was on her shelf unit. It had arrived from him this morning. She had smiled when she saw the label; they were from Fiona Campbell's shop.

Jasmine noticed her looking wistfully at the flowers. 'You are surely not thinking of getting back together?'

Kate looked thoughtful. 'Luke's been very kind these last few days.'

Jasmine frowned. 'Sorry, didn't mean to pry. I don't suppose he mentioned that Glennis finished with him?'

Kate slowly shook her head. 'No, he didn't. How long ago was it?'

'Last week; it was at the squash club. They had a blazing row after she accused him of cheating on her.'

'Now it figures. Man with damaged ego seeks refuge with his estranged wife.' She sighed heavily. 'I, silly fool, thought he still loved me.'

'I'm sorry – I shouldn't have said anything,' said Jasmine with a pout.

Kate's face flushed with colour. 'No, I'm so glad you did, but let's not mention his name again. I'm dying to hear what Tamara's ex-boyfriend said about her. I hope you were discreet.'

'Of course. I gave him a story about Tamara being rude to one of my friends at the nightclub. Turns out her surname is Dunne and she's from Northern Ireland. She told him that she came over with family about seven years ago. He said they met at a party in Radford and shared a spliff. They went out for about three months, then Tamara dumped him. Apparently, it came as a big relief. She didn't just do drugs; she was dealing them. He was too frightened of her to call it off himself.'

'When did she finish with him?'

'About nine months ago. She'd just started working at the Dancing Magpie.'

'Does he know where she lives?'

'She was living on Gregory Boulevard when they met, but he thinks she's moved now. He told me not to go near her; apparently, he's still carrying the scars.'

'Did he say what happened?'

'No, I got the clear impression he didn't want to talk about it. But he did say that Tamara was prone to fits of temper. Something happened to her "Da" that she could never forgive. She had her arm tattooed with a Celtic cross in his memory.'

Kate sipped more of her wine while taking it all in. *Matt and I have been attacked by the same family. Tamara and Gerry are brother and sister.* She was staring into the space between her and Jasmine, unable to focus.

'Kate, are you alright?'

'Sorry… yes. I can't thank you enough for helping.'

Jasmine's pretty nose crinkled a little. 'I have to say I'm worried about you. You've just been assaulted, and now you're going after a psychopath.'

Kate was touched by her friend's concern, but she didn't want her upset so tried her best to seem relaxed. 'Don't be silly. Matt and I know how to handle ourselves. The police are on full alert too.'

'I hope he's paying you well,' said Jasmine, getting to her feet. 'We must do this again. I'm sorry if I've upset you.'

Promising to stay in touch, Kate walked her friend down the stairs from the apartment, past the plain-clothes officer loitering in the lobby and into the car park. When she had waved her off, she hurried back to her flat, picked up the phone and dialled Matt's home number.

'Matt, it's me.'

'You do realise it's the weekend, Kate. Are you okay?'

'Yes, this couldn't wait. My friend's been in touch about Tamara. You'll want to hear this.'

Kate delivered a summary of her meet-up with Jasmine. The excitement she felt made her talk faster. When she finished, there was silence on the line for what seemed to her like minutes but was probably only five seconds.

'Who would have thought it? Tamara and Gerry are siblings. Mrs Brooks, you are… brilliant.'

Matt's reaction emboldened her. 'Do I feel a pay rise coming on?'

'Given the perilous state of our finances, you may have to wait a while. I've got some good news for you though. The café owner recognised Gerry, and I've discovered that he and Tamara gave the keys to River Haven to a homeless guy.'

'Really?'

'I don't think it was planned or even out of charity. Probably they just wanted to throw suspicion on someone else.'

'Who is this guy?'

'His name's Dave. I tracked him down for a chat and I think he's telling me the truth. His story checks out with what the café owner told me. We need to keep our focus on the Dunnes.'

'I agree,' said Kate emphatically. 'What's your take on them?'

'We know Tamara's dealing, so the chances are Toomey's supplying her and she's got customers at Shanahan's club.

Of course, we still need to figure out where Steve Mackie and Colin Mason come into it all.'

'A drugs deal that went bad?' she asked.

'It's possible. Let's see what Greavesie digs up… oh… and the police of course. Maybe it's time I paid my old friend Joe Martin another visit.'

# FORTY

Central Police Station, 3pm: Joe Martin cleared the whisky bottle and glass from his desk into a draw. Then he covered his in-tray with an A4 notepad and moved a plate with the remnants of a bacon cob onto the filing cabinet behind him. He heard footsteps on the uncarpeted corridor and soon the duty sergeant came into sight, Matt Crawford following closely behind. Joe got up and shook the detective's hand, ushering him to a chair as the sergeant left the room.

'Mr Crawford, please take a seat.'

'How's it going, Joe?' asked Matt. 'Saw you on the box last night. Good job.'

The DI wiped his sweaty forehead with his fingers. 'We've been inundated with calls since the newscast. I expect half of them will be bogus and the rest will probably lead nowhere. Still, it will keep the DCS happy. He hauled me in yesterday; told me I needed to smarten up my act.' He gave a throaty, sarcastic chuckle and rocked back in his chair. 'So, today I'm wearing a suit and tie. You said you had some news. It better be good.'

'I think I've found the man who attacked my assistant.'

'Tell me more, young man,' said the inspector, leaning in closer. 'What makes you think you've identified him?'

'When Kate gave me a description, it fitted with a guy I'd come across at the Montague club. He's a bouncer there. Turns out he's an Irishman called Gerry Dunne.'

'That name's familiar,' said Joe, pulling his bottom lip down with his finger. 'Seem to remember we hauled him in a while back. If I recall, he picked a fight with a student.'

'There's more, Joe. The café owner at the marina saw Gerry Dunne and his sister with a homeless guy the morning after the murders. Last night when I met him, he told me that Gerry and his sister Tamara gave him the keys to River Haven that day. His name's Dave and I can tell you where he drinks.'

The DI stroked his chin. 'I'll take the details from you in a moment. Tell me more about the sister.'

'That's interesting too. She's a barmaid at the Dancing Magpie.'

DI Martin's eyes lit up. 'Shanahan's place.'

'How did it go with him?' asked Matt.

'Not well I'm afraid,' said the DI, with a shake of the head. 'His fancy lawyer made sure of that. Still, we've ruffled his feathers, so let's see what his next move is.'

'Got any prints from the house or the van yet?'

'We're working on it. As far as the van goes, forensics

have matched the paint with the fragments that were found on the grass verge near the riverbank.'

'That's positive.'

'Suppose so, but we're still a million miles away from finding out what happened to these guys. Got anything more for me?'

'Isn't that enough?'

'It certainly helps; before you go, son, there is one more thing.'

'What's that?'

'Had a visit from one of Steve Mackie's friends the other day. Name of Harry Barton. I gather you know him.'

'Yes, we've met. Bit of a sad story.'

'What do you make of Mr Barton?' asked the inspector.

'He didn't have a high opinion of Steve. His wife seems protective, and he dotes on his young daughter.' Matt paused for a moment before asking a question he already knew the answer to. 'Why did he come to you?'

'Mr Barton had some information about a fatal crash he and Steve were involved in two years back.'

Matt faked an incredulous stare. 'Really?'

The inspector edged forwards in his chair, lowering his voice. 'Between you and me, he's admitted lying to the police about what happened. I'm considering a prosecution.'

'It speaks well of him that he came forward,' said Matt.

'Yes, I suppose there is that, but as you know, we don't take too kindly to anyone perverting the course of justice.'

'But I know as well as you do that we don't always have to play it by the book. What did he tell you exactly?'

DI Martin cleared his throat. 'I can't disclose that right now.'

'Does it have a bearing on the murder cases?' asked Matt, his eyebrows raised.

The policeman didn't give an answer, merely a shrug of the shoulders.

DI Martin took more details from Matt about the witnesses and Tamara before showing him downstairs. He came back to his office feeling uneasy. Slumping back into his chair, he took off his suit jacket and loosened his tie. He pulled out the glass and bottle from a desk drawer and poured himself a large one. *Nothing like a whisky to take the edge off a rough day.* As the inspector swilled the scotch around his mouth, he began to reflect. What he had so far was a bunch of loose ends. One victim killed by a blow to the head, the other by gunshot. No murder weapons found. A stolen van which was at the crime scene. And now, courtesy of Matt Crawford, two new photos to pin up on the incident room board, two more suspects to question. He still had a lot more questions than answers. Why were Mackie and Mason killed and what connected them? Who had a grudge against them? Was it for money, or some other reason?

He was suddenly aware of the ticking of the clock on the wall. Time was not his friend. With each minute, hour and day, the murderer's trail was getting colder, and the heat was turned up on him and his team. There was something else troubling him too. Something he hadn't told Matt. When the DCS had called him in, he'd asked who was leading this murder inquiry, 'You, DI Martin, or a two-bit private eye?'

Joe thumped his empty glass down on the desk, sprang out of his chair and headed down the corridor to find his DS.

\*\*\*

On their way to the Dancing Magpie, DS Crowther told his boss how sad it was that a magnificent nineteenth-century lace mill had been cannibalised into a nightclub. Joe Martin let the younger officer lead the way as they flashed their cards at the heavy manning the main door and made their way along the side of the empty dance floor. It was still another hour to opening time. Behind the bar was a woman fitting the description Matt had given Joe earlier: punk hairstyle, black T-shirt and face with an attitude. She was doing her best to pretend to be busy wiping down the beer taps as they approached. Now Joe took over, signalling for the younger officer to take notes.

'We're looking for a Tamara Dunne. That wouldn't happen to be you, would it?' he asked.

'Who's asking?' she said without looking up.

'We're police officers,' said DI Martin, holding his identity card under her nose to get her attention.

She gave a snort. 'That's my name. What's this about?'

'Your boss has been helping us with our inquiries. We are investigating the murders of Steve Mackie and Colin Mason.'

Tamara pinched her nose. 'What's that got to do with me? I just work behind the bar for him; I ain't done nothing wrong.'

'In that case,' said Joe, 'I'm sure you won't mind answering a few questions. Let's start with where you were on the evening of Wednesday, 23 March.'

She put a hand on her hip. 'That's a while back. Might have been working… I dunno.'

'We'll need you to tell us exactly where you were and who you were with,' said Joe, with a stern face. 'Another thing,' he said, 'did you know either of these men?'

'No,' she replied.

'You sure? They weren't customers here?'

'Not that I know of. All I've seen of them is their photos in the papers.'

'Did your brother know them?' asked Joe.

She ran her hand through her spikey hair. 'Gerry? Don't think so.'

'Know where we might find Gerry tonight?'

'Some nights he works on the door at the Montague. If he's not there, he might be drinking at Yates Wine Lodge.'

'Thank you. That's probably all we need, for now anyway. But we do have to ask you to come by the station. Shall we say Monday morning at 10am? Maybe by then you'll have remembered where you were on the night of the twenty-third. There'll be a few more routine questions we'll need to go through with you. It's the police station on Shakespeare Street. Just ask for me or DS Crowther when you get there. Have a good evening and give Mr Shanahan my regards when you see him.'

# DAY FOURTEEN

Sunday, 10 April 1983

# FORTY-ONE

The rain of recent days had given way to pastel blue skies streaked with wispy clouds. Matt had driven his Beetle, windows down and music loud, along the wide expanse of London Road past the green-roofed council buildings in West Bridgford. At traffic lights, he forked left, drove past Fiona's flower shop and then turned right into Hazel's street. It was a narrow cul-de-sac of 1930's houses with white rendered, half-timbered frontages. He parked outside her house, which had a low wall to the front and a wrought-iron gate. His rusty VW looked a little out of place among the well-polished family saloons parked around it. He paused at the gate and scanned the street north and south. But for a young family of four out walking in their Sunday best, there was nobody to be seen. He unlatched the gate and approached the front door. Just as he was poised to push the bell, it sprang open, and Hazel ushered him in. She had been watching him through the net curtains.

The first thing he noticed in the lounge was the absence of condolence cards and flowers. There were no family photos on show either. There were Royal Doulton figurines on the mantelpiece, and holiday brochures were spread across the coffee table.

'Going anywhere nice?' he asked, pointing to them.

'It's my sister's idea. Anywhere but Menorca I told her. That was our last holiday together.'

'Still leaves plenty of options, and it's probably just what you need.'

'I suppose I am tired of being surrounded by constant reminders of Steve.'

'Have the police been in touch?'

'The liaison officer dropped by three days ago to check I hadn't fled the country. Other than that, no.'

'You saw the news conference?'

'Yes, for what it's worth,' she said with a shrug. 'More of a PR exercise to keep the press happy if you ask me. I don't like that man.'

'Joe Martin's not everyone's cup of tea, but he's trustworthy.'

'He's suspicious of me, I know it. Anyway, you said you had some news?'

'More of an update really. We've found two persons of interest who were at the marina the day Steve died.'

She became flushed. 'There we go again. *You* found them, not slow and steady Joe. See what I mean? He's a complete waste of time. Who are these people?'

'Ever heard of Gerry Dunne or his sister? She's called

Tamara, but her friends call her Tammy.'

She wound a dark curl of hair around a finger. 'No, never heard of either of them.'

'What about Mel Toomey? Did his name ever come up?'

'I can't say it's familiar. You said two people; how does he come into it?'

'Mr Toomey was one of Steve's poker buddies.'

'Does this mean you no longer think it's that nightclub owner... Shanahan?'

'No, it doesn't. He might still be the one we're looking for. There is something else, though. Kate has been attacked.'

Hazel's mouth gaped. 'Kate? How is she?'

'She's okay now. Still got a bit of a sore head.'

'When did this happen?'

'Four days ago.'

'You didn't say—'

'I didn't want to alarm you. She's fine.'

'You think it's connected to the murders?' she asked, tilting her head.

'Almost certainly. We're pretty sure it was the guy I mentioned just now, Gerry Dunne.'

'Matt, I will quite understand if you wish to step down.'

'No. Both Kate and I want to see this through. But if *you've* had second thoughts...'

Her jaw stiffened. 'I want Steve's murderer found. You are my best bet, Matt... if anything, I think I should be paying you more. Please send Kate my best wishes. Is she back at work?'

His laugh was more of a grunt. 'I couldn't keep her away.'

Hazel put her hand to her mouth. 'I'm sorry, I didn't even offer you a drink. Will you stay for a coffee or maybe something stronger?'

Matt was very tempted, but then reminded himself of his golden rule. 'That's kind, but I have to be going.'

Hazel chewed her lip. 'No doubt you've got better things to do with your time. By the way, how's it going with Fiona? I heard you had drinks the other night.'

His face reddened. 'She told you?'

'She let it slip at her dinner party on Friday. I think she likes you.'

\*\*\*

In the quiet of a Sunday evening in his flat, thoughts of Fiona were still in Matt's head as he sat at the kitchen table drinking Scotch and picking at a packet of salted peanuts. The night with Fiona, fabulously good-looking though she was, served as a reminder of past mistakes. She was a lot like Amanda: self-assured, aware of her beauty and full of drama. Maybe making love to her was a kind of revenge trip on his part. He would have to find a way of letting her down gently. He knew just the person who could help him with this.

He put down his glass, went to the phone in the hall and dialled his brother's number. Richard sounded upbeat. 'I was wondering when you'd ring. Did DI Martin call you?'

'No, I was ringing about something else. What's happened?' asked Matt.

'Forensics have reported again on the van; there are fingerprints which are a match for your Gerry Dunne.'

'Wow, that's great,' said Matt.

'Yes, Joe Martin's in buoyant mood. It's the breakthrough he's been waiting for.'

'It puts Gerry Dunne in the van that was seen by the neighbour outside River Haven on the day of the murders.'

'But it's still a long way from proving he was involved in murder,' said Richard.

'Agreed, but we're getting closer. The paint fragments I found that put the van at the crime scene. And there's more. Did Joe tell you that I've found a witness who saw Gerry Dunne and his sister at the marina on the day after the murders? They gave the keys to River Haven to a homeless guy who I've now tracked down.'

'No, he must have conveniently forgotten to mention it.'

'Of course, why would he?' said Matt, with more than a hint of sarcasm.

There was a brief silence on the line before Richard spoke again. His voice sounded a little croaky. 'Matt... I must say something now. Our dad would have been very proud of you at this moment. You are a huge loss to the force. Now, what was it you wanted to ask me?'

'Oh that... I just needed some brotherly advice, but it can wait.'

# DAY FIFTEEN

Monday, 11 April 1983

# FORTY-TWO

Central Police Station, 9.30am: He wiped a bead of sweat from his forehead with his hand. The ceiling lights hung low and seemed to be burning into his skin. The bare magnolia walls and lack of carpets made the place feel more like a prison cell than an interview room. His solicitor, James Wallace, sat to his left; he wore horn-rimmed glasses and a smart grey suit. Opposite him sat DI Joe Martin, whom he recognised from the TV, and a younger policeman with a pimpled face, introduced as DS Crowther. Gerry leant back in his chair, trying to look relaxed, and waited for the show to begin. *Give them nothing,* he said to himself, *they will make out they know more than they do. They'll try to trap me.*

The DS held a blue ballpoint pen poised over a clean A4 notepad. The inspector picked up a brown file from the desk and held it up so that its contents were hidden from Gerry. He began to thumb through the papers inside it. As he did so, he let out an occasional tut and a shake of the head. After what seemed like fifteen minutes, but was probably less than three, he closed the file and laid it back on the desk. Now he looked Gerry directly in the eyes.

'I'll be frank, Mr Dunne, it doesn't look good for you from where I'm sitting.'

*Heard that one before. I'm not as stupid as they think I am. Don't say a word.*

The DI edged forwards in his chair. 'You *do* know why we've brought you here, don't you?'

Gerry glanced across at his solicitor and shrugged his shoulders.

'Three weeks ago, on 23 March to be precise, two men were murdered at Beeston Marina. Steve Mackie and Colin Mason. I, for one, can't even begin to imagine the devastating effect this has had on their families.'

*Well I can*, thought Gerry, *my own da was gunned down in cold blood by one of your fecking uniforms.*

The inspector opened the file, took out a photograph and slid it across the table. 'This man is Steve Mackie. Did you know him?'

Gerry gave the photo a cursory glance. 'Can't say as I *knew* the bloke, but I've seen him once or twice at the club.'

'The Montague club?' asked the DI. Gerry confirmed this with a nod of the head.

'We understand you are a doorman there. Is that right?'

'Yes.'

'Been there long?' asked the inspector.

'Three years.'

DI Martin took a second photo from the file and held it up. 'And this man, Colin Mason. Did you know him too?'

Gerry paused to take a close look at the creased black-and-white snapshot. 'No, never seen him before.'

'Where were you on the evening of Wednesday, 23 March?' asked the inspector.

'Can't say for sure. Probably at work.'

'Maybe this will jog your memory. You were seen at Beeston Marina the next morning, with your sister.'

Gerry fidgeted with his shirt collar; his neck was getting warm. 'Ah yes, now I remember. We'd gone for a walk along the canal the next morning and stopped at the café for a coffee. It's a nice spot there, so it is. Tamara stayed over the night before and cooked a meal. We were at my place all evening.'

'Your sister can vouch for you? That's convenient,' said the DI with a raised eyebrow. 'We'll ask her ourselves. She's waiting for us now in fact, just down the corridor.'

Gerry was grinding his teeth. 'You've no business talking to her. Tamara's not involved in any of this.'

'Meaning *you* are?' said DI Martin.

James Wallace peered over his glasses, a supercilious look on his face. 'Inspector, my client has told you where he was when these murders took place. Now, if that's all—'

'No, it certainly isn't. I have something else to show you.' The DI took another photo from the folder and placed it next to the others. 'Recognise these, Mr Dunne?'

'It's a set of keys,' said Gerry with a weak smile.

'They belong to the house Steve Mackie was selling on

Meadow Road, a house called River Haven. He arranged to meet Colin Mason there the day they were both killed.'

Wallace gave the inspector a confused look. 'What has this got to do with my client?'

'We have a witness who says that Mr Dunne gave him these keys the very next day, at the café at Beeston Marina. Perhaps he can explain how he came by them?'

Gerry shot a glance at his solicitor before replying, 'Whoever told you this is lying to save their own skin. I never had any keys.'

DI Martin gave Gerry a cold stare. 'We'll find out soon enough who's been lying to us. Here's another picture for you.' He slid it across the table. 'Recognise this vehicle?'

Gerry shook his head. 'Nope.'

The inspector smiled. 'You should do. We've found your fingerprints on it. It was stolen a few weeks back. We also know that the number plates were switched. This van was seen outside River Haven the day Steve Mackie was murdered. We can also prove it was near the scene of both murders, close to the riverbank. Are you sure you've never seen it before, Mr Dunne?'

Wallace interjected quickly. 'My client has no comment.'

'I expected as much. Why did you kill these men, Mr Dunne? Who put you up to it? Was it your sister? Or her boss, Mr Shanahan?'

Wallace held up his hand. 'This is utterly ridiculous. My client has already told you he has an alibi. What reason could he possibly have for killing these two men? You are making wild accusations with not one iota of evidence to support them.'

DI Martin gave him a wry smile. 'I beg to differ, Mr Wallace, but let's move on. Six days ago, a woman was assaulted. Her name is Kate Brooks; she's a private detective working for Steve Mackie's widow. The description she gave of her attacker fits yours, Mr Dunne. Why did you hurt her? Was it a warning to back off the case?'

'I don't know what you're talking about; I never hurt anyone,' said Gerry in a low, monotone voice.

Joe Martin's face was a fiery red. 'Really? Here's the thing. I don't believe a single word you've said today. Not one syllable. Mr Dunne, I'm arresting you on suspicion of two counts of murder and one of assault. DS Crowther, please escort these two gentlemen down to the cells and read the accused his rights.'

\*\*\*

Two doors down the corridor, Tamara was leaning against the bare wall of the interview room, hands in pockets. The mug of tea they'd brought her earlier had been left to go cold on the table. *Shanahan was wrong, Crawford must have recognised me. So what? His word against mine, and Gerry will be my alibi. I'm too bloody soft, that's my trouble. Gerry would have finished the job. An eye for an eye, that's what Gerry says. They've no fecking clue what it was like over there. Thrown out of our own home and left on the streets just for being Catholic. We'd lived side by side for all those years with our Protestant neighbours without any bother. Then when me da takes to the streets to stand up for his family, he is shot down. They would have taken more pity on a rabid dog, the bloody police. What business have they calling themselves "Royal"? They are nothing but butchers. Father Anthony said we should try to forgive and forget. He doesn't mean it. He just wants to stop me feeling angry. He's boiling up inside too, I know it. I can't get the war out of my head. I've tried, but the pictures are still there. Barbed wire, tanks, soldiers, police. Our belongings thrown onto the street like rubbish for collection.*

Her thoughts were interrupted by a knock on the door. A WPC ushered in a smart-suited man with greying hair, carrying a leather briefcase. He walked towards her and shook her hand.

'Miss Dunne, I'm your solicitor, William Franklin. Mr Toomey said you might be needing my services today.'

# FORTY-THREE

The Flying Horse, 1pm: over a pint of bitter, Matt was struggling to solve the *Daily Telegraph* crossword he'd started earlier. Six across was giving him trouble: "Cult adopting unique selling point is dubious" – seven letters. *Richard's the cryptic crossword king. Would have done the whole thing by now.* As he pondered on his older brother's superiority, a shadow appeared over his table, making him look up. It was his old friend.

'What can I get you, Greavesie?' he asked, getting up from his chair.

'Pint of Guinness and a packet of Walkers, salt and vinegar.'

Matt came back to the table with the drink and crisps to find Greavesie studying his crossword. 'Stuck, are you?'

'I suspect so. Wait a minute, that's the answer – SUSPECT – cheers Greavesie!'

They clinked glasses. 'Cheers. This is the best Guinness in town, by the way.'

'Glad to hear it. My pint will taste all the better if you've found something on Toomey. What have you got for me?'

Greavesie put down his glass and lowered his voice. 'An interesting bloke, your Mr Toomey. Did you know he owns the big Italian restaurant on Maid Marion Way? Word on the street is that he's using it to "launder" the cash from his drugs empire.'

'I didn't know that, Greavesie, well done. What else did you find?'

'Seems he's looking for other hiding places for his illegal earnings.'

'Like where?'

'He's recently got into property development.'

Matt's eyes lit up. 'Tell me more.'

There was a pause while his friend chewed on a crisp. 'There's a new housing scheme in Stapleford he's put money into. Guess who his business partner is? Mackie Estates in West Bridgford.'

Matt raised his glass towards his friend. 'Greavesie, you're a bloody genius.'

It was unusual to see his friend crack such a broad smile. 'That's not quite everything,' said Greavesie. 'He's shacked up in a big country house in Normanton-on-the-Wolds. It's called The Grange. As far as I've heard, there is no Mrs Toomey at present, although he is not short of female guests.'

'Think I owe you another drink after that.'

Greavesie raised his hand. 'Sorry, can't stop much

longer. Got an appointment with my accountant – *turf* accountant that is.'

Matt slid a hand into his jacket pocket and pulled out a fat brown envelope. He slipped it across the table. 'Thanks, mate. I won't forget this. Can you just do one more thing for me?'

His friend looked curious. 'What's that?'

'Pay it into your bank before you get to the bookies.'

\*\*\*

Matt was back in the office talking things through with Kate over tea and biscuits. The conversation turned to his ex-wife's new fiancé.

'Seems that Guy Travers forgot to mention that Steve Mackie had a partner,' said Matt.

'Strange that, isn't it?' said Kate, with a smirk. 'Especially as it was someone so eminent and trustworthy.'

Matt huffed. 'I'm wondering if Toomey is one of Guy Travers' clients. Check it out, will you?'

'Will do. Do you think Travers is involved too?'

'He needs looking into.'

She peered up at him. 'You don't have ulterior motives, I hope?'

He raised his voice. 'What, because he's shacked up with my ex-wife? No, I would never make it personal; that's not professional.'

Her face reddened. 'Sorry, I shouldn't have even suggested it.'

'Apology accepted. Now, I'd like to bounce some thoughts off you if you're ready.'

She stopped sipping her tea and put the mug down. 'Bounce away.'

'I'm thinking that Steve Mackie and Toomey might have had a big falling out.'

'Over what?'

'That's what we need to find out. Their property scheme, a gambling debt or a drugs deal maybe?'

Kate bit on a chocolate digestive and was still chewing as she spoke. 'That would figure. And we know when Mr Toomey is displeased…'

Matt swiped his index finger across his throat. 'Exactly. Here's one theory I have. We know that Tammy Dunne is one of his dealers. So, what if Toomey pays big money for her and her big brother to kill Steve?'

'Seems plausible,' said Kate, brushing a biscuit crumb off her blouse. 'And with Steve out of the way, Toomey would be confident of buying out his widow and taking all of the profits.'

'Yes, that all adds up. But a couple of things are still troubling me.'

'Go on.'

'Number one. Hazel seems very keen to leave the country. She had holiday brochures strewn all over the lounge.'

'You still think she could be involved?' asked Kate.

Matt looked thoughtful. 'I'm not ruling it out. He lied to her, and he cheated on her. She had every reason to hate him.'

'But then, why is she so set on finding the killer? You think it's all a bluff?'

'I'm just saying it's possible that this is not about

money. Maybe it's a crime of passion.'

'Then, what about Ellie Price?' said Kate. 'She had every reason to be angry too. He took her money and drove her son to his death. And someone definitely took offence to us contacting her.'

'Could be they were protecting her, using Gerry Dunne as the muscle. You're right, we can't rule her out either. We need to talk to her again.'

'You mentioned *two* things?' she asked.

'Ah yes, that brings me to Colin Mason,' he sighed. 'Any thoughts on where he might fit into all of this?'

She ran her hand through her curls. 'They used him to lure Steve to the house. Once he'd done his part, he was a liability.'

'That would make a lot of sense. But we still have no murder weapon and no proof and that's—'

'The hard bit,' she said, with a grin.

He affected a posh accent. 'Precisely, my dear Mrs Brooks. So, when you've quite finished that biscuit, there's work to do. See what you can get from Guy Travers.' He stood up from his chair. 'I'll catch you later.'

She did a double take. 'Where are you off to this time?'

'City life is beginning to get me down,' he said, fidgeting with his shirt collar. 'I'm finding it a bit claustrophobic. Thought I might take the car for a run in the countryside and take in the scenery.'

# FORTY-FOUR

After a windows-down sprint through country roads in his Beetle, Matt reached Normanton-on-the-Wolds and parked close to the Plough Inn. The Grange was only five minutes' walk away. It was a white rendered cottage with a long, curved gravel drive, well-trimmed privet hedges and flower beds full of rose bushes. His shoes scuffed through the small stones as he walked up the drive, passing a gleaming black Mercedes on his way to the door. There were Roman columns on either side of the entrance. The doorbell was set in marble to the right of a solid oak door. Soon after he rang it, he heard a man's voice shout that the door needed answering. A minute later, it opened, and a tall woman in her forties with an orange tan and a leopard-print blouse appeared. She fluttered her false eyelashes at him.

'If you're here to do the garden, it's the side gate.'

'No, I'm not,' said Matt, pulling out his calling card from his jacket pocket and handing it to her. 'Tell Mr Toomey I'd like a quick word. We're old acquaintances.'

She held the card in both hands and squinted at the small print. 'Afraid he's not in, Mr Crawford.'

Matt gave her an icy glare. 'Don't give me that tosh, I heard him just now. Just tell him, will you?'

'Wait here,' she said drily, then turned, shutting the heavy door with a loud clunk.

Matt stepped away from the porch and scanned the front of the house. There were security cameras at each corner and over the garage doors. There was loud birdsong coming from the back of the house. He walked towards the wrought-iron side gate. Looking through it, he could see the massive extent of the rear garden, laid out mostly to lawn. In the nearest flower bed, he spotted a white statue of a Greek goddess with water trickling from an urn she was carrying under her arm. A blackbird was perched on top of her head. The sweet sound of its song was interrupted by the crunching of footsteps on the gravel. Turning around, he came face to face with the owner. Mel Toomey looked older than Matt remembered; his thick crop of hair was white, as was his well-trimmed beard.

'Long time no see,' said Toomey, the ghost of a smile on his pallid face. 'What's eating you?'

Matt shrugged his shoulders. 'Just fancied a change of scene and some country air. Nice place you've got here; business must be booming. Hear you're into property now.'

'But you're not here to discuss real estate, are you?' said Toomey, with a sarcastic grin.

'In a way I am. Your estate agent friend Steve Mackie, know who killed him?'

Toomey's nostrils flared. 'You think *I* had something to do with it? I'm sorry to disappoint you, but I didn't.'

'He was your business partner. Maybe you had a disagreement?'

'No way,' said Toomey.

'Know anyone who bore him a grudge?'

'Never mentioned anyone to me,' said Toomey in a flat voice.

'Did he owe you money?'

'No.'

'Know *Mrs* Mackie, do you?'

'No, never had that pleasure.'

'Guess you will soon enough. She'll want to know all about the deal her husband mortgaged their house for. I suppose, with Steve no longer on the scene, you'll be wanting to buy her out?'

Toomey shook his head. 'You've got me all wrong, son. Now, if that's all, I must ask you to leave now.'

'Just one more thing before I go. Colin Mason, what do you know about him?'

'The stiff they pulled out of the river. Nothing.'

'Was he a friend of Steve's?'

'Never heard him mention that name. Now, I really do have to be going.'

Matt looked straight into Toomey's narrow, unblinking eyes. 'You sure you don't know who killed them?'

'I'm not the one you should be asking.'

'Who should I be talking to, then?'

'You're the bloody detective, you work it out. One

thing I know for sure is you're way off the mark here. Why don't you try looking closer to home?'

***

Evening was drawing in when he got back to the office. Kate was at her desk with Desmond curled at her feet. Matt told her about his visit to the Toomey mansion.

'Do you think he's being straight with you?' she asked.

Matt pinched his nose. 'He's hard to read. I still think he's involved.'

'When he said look closer to home,' said Kate, 'whose home did he mean? Yours or Steve's maybe?'

'Your guess is as good as mine. If we are to believe him, the villain is under our noses either way. Anything happen while I was gone?'

'Quite a bit; I've barely been off the phone. Spoke to Guy Travers after you left. He flatly refused to say if Toomey is on his client list.'

He smiled. 'Client confidentiality, I suppose.'

'You got it in one. I asked Travers if he knew how Toomey and Steve had become business partners. He said he thinks they first met at the Montague club.'

'That would figure. Did he say anything else?'

'Not really, but he did ask how the investigation was going.'

'You told him?'

'Of course not, other than some vague remarks about following up some interesting leads.'

'Good girl. Anyone else call?'

'Yes, your brother. He asked you to call back this evening.'

'Good.'

She blushed. 'There is just one more thing. My ex-colleague rang again.'

'Keith Ferrell? What did he want?'

'He says he's got some information for us, about Steve Mackie.'

'Go on.'

'He's going to tell me over dinner tonight.'

Matt's mouth dropped open. 'I thought—'

'A girl can change her mind, can't she?' Kate said with a grin. 'Anyway, who knows, Keith might be onto something.'

# FORTY-FIVE

Later that evening, Matt took a can of lager from the fridge and slumped onto the sofa. Desmond followed him from the kitchen and loped towards the single easy chair. The cat licked his lips before curling up on a cushion, his eyes turned towards his master.

'Don't look at me like that, cat; you can't possibly be hungry after a whole tin of food. Or are you just sulking because Auntie Kate's gone home?'

The cat flapped his ears.

'You're stuck with me I'm afraid; she's not coming back until tomorrow. She's your favourite, isn't she? I know just how you feel because I like her too. Do you think I should tell her how much?'

Desmond purred.

'I'll take that as a yes,' said Matt, snapping the ring-pull and taking a slurp from the can. 'I promise you I will talk to her when the time is right.'

The cat sighed, turned his head to the side and closed his eyes.

Matt drained the rest of his lager, got up from the sofa and walked through to the hall. He dialled his brother's number.

'Hello, Richard, Kate said you called?'

'Yes, there's big news from this end, thought you'd like some advance warning. For your ears only, Gerry and Tamara Dunne have been arrested on suspicion of murder. I think there's going to be a press briefing tomorrow. No names mentioned at this stage.'

'That's great news. I just hope Joe's got all his ducks in a row.'

'You think he might have got it wrong?'

'I don't know. Everything points to the Dunnes, but I'm still struggling to come up with a motive. My guess is someone hired them to do their dirty work.'

'Still convinced Toomey's behind this?' asked Richard.

'You think I want it to be him. Maybe I do in a way. I've just discovered he and Mackie were partners; maybe Steve tried to pull a fast one. Toomey doesn't take very kindly to being cheated out of money.'

'The Dunnes are still in custody. Let's see if they talk.'

After he ended the call, he saw a number scribbled on the notepad by the phone, reminding him there was another call to make. He felt his heart racing as he dialled, half hoping Fiona wouldn't answer, but she did.

'Matt, it's lovely to hear from you.'

'Sorry I couldn't make it the other night.'

'Another time maybe? Are you free next weekend?'

He paused for breath. 'I'm not sure… can we just leave

it for a while? The Mackie case is taking all of my day and some of my nights too.'

There was silence on the line for a few seconds. 'Is there someone else, Matt?'

'No… I just need some time.'

She sighed. 'Okay, you know where to find me when you're ready. Goodnight, Matt.'

He put the phone down, not liking himself for what he'd just done, then headed straight back to the fridge.

\*\*\*

On the other side of the city, Kate took a sip of red wine before taking another mouthful of beef ravioli. Across the table, Keith was wrapping spaghetti around his fork. The busy restaurant was filled with after-work chatter and the aroma of garlic and parmesan cheese. A waiter flitted past their table holding a giant pot of black pepper. In the background, Kate could hear opera music playing. She was finding it difficult to distinguish it above the buzz of conversation, but it sounded like Verdi's *La traviata*.

'Delicious food, Keith. How did you find this place?'

'The boss likes it here.'

'How is he these days?'

'Same old tyrant he always was. How's yours?'

'Matt's very different. I'm well looked after.'

'Are you sure?' he asked, pointing to the plaster at the back of her head. 'Looks like he should be paying you danger money. What happened?'

'I fell… at home.'

He looked sceptical. 'Really? That's not what I heard.'

She smirked. 'That's the problem with you reporters; you listen to too much gossip.'

He chuckled. 'Give me the facts then. Who wanted to hurt you?'

'I told you, it was an accident.'

'Okay, let's move on. How is the investigation going?'

'Nice try, but I'm under strict instructions not to talk about the case – to anyone. You said you had some news of your own?'

Keith lowered his voice. 'I spoke to someone who used to work with Steve Mackie at Harlow's Estate Agents. They said he left under a cloud.'

'How come?'

'They suspected he was taking money on the side from clients to secure cut-price deals.'

'Who told you this?'

'I can't tell you that, but it's a reliable source. And there's more; are you aware that Mackie was involved in a big housing development?'

'Yes, we are, in Stapleford.'

'But did you know that he gazumped another developer? I understand his competitor is still very sore about it. He accused Mackie of bribing the estate agent.'

'When was this?'

'Two weeks before Steve's murder. My source said that the developer stormed out of the agent's offices and swore he'd make "that bastard Mackie" pay for what he'd done.'

Kate slid her chair closer. 'You have a name?'

# DAY SIXTEEN

Tuesday, 12 April 1983

# FORTY-SIX

The Crawford Agency, 9am: Kate brought coffee into Matt's office and settled into a chair facing her boss.

'Made you a strong black one,' she said, placing the steaming mug in front of him.

'Was it *that* obvious?'

'The red eyes and slow walk gave you away. I guess you were in town last night?'

'No, I was at home with Desmond, curled up on the couch. We watched a Clint Eastwood film. How did it go with your old mate Keith Ferrell?'

'He took me to a posh Italian place.'

Matt sipped his drink and winced. 'Not on Maid Marion Way by any chance?'

'Why do you ask?'

'Toomey owns it.'

'You're obsessed with him, aren't you? No, this one was

on Upper Parliament Street. Waiters in dinner suits, silver candelabras on the table and opera music.'

His grin was sarcastic. 'Sounds right up my alley. What was the big scoop he had for you?'

'He's found someone who had a bone to pick with Steve Mackie.'

'Really? Who?'

'A property developer called Ken Marchant. His office is just two minutes' walk from here.'

Matt stroked his unshaven chin. 'I've heard the name before. When I was at River Haven with her, Monica mentioned that Marchant had called in at the office around the time Steve disappeared. I was so intent on poking around in the house that I let it slip my mind until now.'

'Apparently Mr Marchant got very irate when he was outbid by Mackie on the site in Stapleford. He thinks Mackie greased someone's palms.'

'Oiling the wheels of commerce, I think they call it,' said Matt with a wry grin.

'I'm wondering if that's what Toomey meant when he said we needed to look closer to home. Marchant is practically on our doorstep.'

'Could be, though I wouldn't put it past Toomey to send us up the wrong path to deflect attention from himself. Let's have a word with Mr Marchant. Let's see what he has to say about Steve Mackie. Perhaps the gentle touch is what's needed here. Think you can handle it?'

'Yes, I'll get right over there. Will you be holding the fort?'

'No, I'm going to leave Desmond in charge. It's high

time that cat earned his keep. What's more, my Beetle needs a run. Thought I'd take a drive out to Beeston.'

\*\*\*

They sat in his office on the first floor of a Victorian brick building with large casement windows that cast a bright, natural light. City traffic rumbled by in the background. Ken Marchant was a short, muscular man in his forties with a deep suntan. His white open-necked shirt revealed too many chest hairs for her liking.

'My secretary said you wanted some information about Steve Mackie.'

Kate crossed her legs and rested her notepad on her lap. 'That's right. We are working for his widow, Hazel. How well did you know him?'

'Hardly at all. Met him a couple of times when he was at Harlow's.'

'Harlow's?' she asked.

'The estate agents in West Bridgford. He used to work there, along with his sidekick, Monica Purvis.'

She looked him straight in the eyes. 'You called at his office recently. Would you like to tell me what that was about?'

Marchant cleared his throat. 'A courtesy call. I was interested to know how the Stapleford scheme was coming on.'

'Your own bid failed I understand.'

He frowned. 'Sadly, yes. Property's a cut-throat business.'

'I'm told you were very angry about losing the contract. Doesn't sound like a courtesy call to me. Why were you there Mr Marchant?'

He stayed silent for a moment. 'Alright, I wanted to give him a piece of my mind. But he wasn't there.'

'Were you surprised to hear about his murder?'

'Not really, if I'm honest. Steve kept bad company.'

She affected bemusement. 'How do you mean?'

'Poker players and drugs dealers.'

'Can you give me any names?'

Marchant fidgeted with his gold neck chain. 'Michael Shanahan and Mel Toomey.'

'Wasn't Mr Toomey his business partner?'

'Partner in crime more like. Bribery and corruption's the name of the game.'

'Sounds to me like you're still bitter about what happened.'

He gave her a wry smile. 'I see where this is leading. Yes, I did say some things about Mackie in the heat of the moment but, believe me, I would never harm a living soul.'

'Can you think of anyone who might?'

'I've already mentioned two of them. Steve Mackie was out of his depth, simple as that.'

# FORTY-SEVEN

Ellie had greeted him at her door with a strained smile. She wore a plain black blouse, buttoned at the neck, and a long grey skirt. It seemed she was always trying to counteract her good looks with her drab clothes, as if it were a sin to look attractive. They sat sharing a pot of tea in her front room, warmed by a flickering fire.

'I'm guessing you have some news for me,' said Ellie with a nervous smile.

'As a matter of fact, I do. Two suspects have been arrested in connection with the murders.'

'Who are they?' she asked.

*Can't tell her now. She'll find out soon enough.* 'That we don't know yet. The police have them in custody and we can expect an update from them soon.'

'I'm relieved. The longer it drags on the worse I feel. Not knowing what happened to Steve and why.' She ran her finger around the rim of the teacup. 'Does that mean your work is finished?'

'Only if the police have got the right people.'

'You still have your doubts?' she said, raising an eyebrow.

'I suppose I do. Kate thinks I'm the ultimate sceptic.'

Ellie gave a deep sigh. 'I'm sorry, I should have asked you this before. How is she?'

'Still a little sore in the head but back at work.'

'I'm sorry she had such bad luck. It's normally so quiet around here.'

'I doubt it was a mugging. You see, we got a threatening letter too. It seems somebody didn't want her talking to you. Can you think of a reason why?'

'I swear to God, I can't,' she said, touching the crucifix which dangled on a silver chain over her breast.

'You said that Steve talked to you about the housing scheme in Stapleford. Did he ever mention any of his business friends? Do the names Mel Toomey and Michael Shanahan mean anything to you?'

'I'm afraid not,' she said, placing her empty cup down on the table. 'Steve never mentioned either of them to me.'

'What about Ken Marchant?'

'Never heard his name either.'

'Are you certain?'

'Yes, quite certain. Now, if that's all, Mr Crawford, I must be getting along. There's a church coffee morning I need to get to. I'll see you out.'

Ellie got up from her chair and Matt followed her towards the door. His keen eye was taken by a small photo hanging to the left of it, and he paused in the doorway to take a closer look. It had been taken on the front doorstep of the church. Ellie and another middle-aged woman wore flowery aprons. They were flanked by Father Anthony Moss in his priest's gown and a tall man wearing overalls. Matt recognised him at once. When Ellie turned round to see where he was, Matt pointed to the photo.

'It was taken at the church fete last summer,' said Ellie.

'Who is the man in the overalls? He seems vaguely familiar.'

'That's Gerry, a friend of Father Anthony's. He does the gardens and helps with odd jobs at the church.'

'Know much about him?'

'Father Anthony knew his family back in Belfast. When their father died in a shooting a few years back, he helped Gerry and his sister with their move over here. Put them up in his own house for a while. He treats Gerry like the son he never had.'

'And his sister?'

'Tamara? We don't see much of her. Bit of a wild child by all accounts. She'll probably grow out of it.'

***

Kate was on the phone when he got back to the office. 'Hold on a moment, Inspector, he's just walked in. I'll hand you over.'

She handed the receiver to Matt. 'Hello, Joe, how's it going?'

'We are making progress. What I'm telling you now is in the strictest confidence. We have arrested Gerry and Tamara Dunne on suspicion of murder.'

'That was fast work,' he said, sounding as excited as he could about old news.

'They are both denying it of course. But the evidence is compelling. We found their prints on the van and hairs found on Steve Mackie's clothing are a match for Gerry Dunne. We also found a length of rope in the van which is a perfect match for the rope marks on Steve Mackie's wrists. It's mooring rope, the same as we found at the house.'

'Have you established motive?' asked Matt.

'No. That's what is bothering me.'

'You think they were hired?'

'Could be. Neither of them is talking much, but I sense we may get more out of the sister. Maybe we can cut a deal with her.'

'Don't go too soft on her, Joe. I have strong reason to believe that she's the one that stabbed me when I was trying to bust Toomey.'

'She stabbed you? Why didn't you tell me this before?'

'I have no real proof, other than recognising the tattoo on her arm and pock marks on her face.'

'What connection does she have to Toomey?'

'She's one of his dealers.'

'We'll do some digging. I'd better be off now. Got to talk to our friends from the press and TV.'

'What are you going to tell them?'

'The bare minimum. That we've made two arrests in connection with the murders, and we'll keep them informed of developments.'

Matt thanked Joe and put the receiver down. 'I suppose you heard most of that?' he said to Kate. 'What do you make of it?'

'Seems pretty conclusive, although the question of motive is still unanswered.'

'Exactly, my dear Brooks. Everything points to them being hired. How did you get on with Marchant by the way?'

'Says he's not the killing kind. Pointed the finger at Shanahan and Toomey.'

'Do you believe him?' asked Matt.

'You know what? I probably do. How did you get on in Beeston?'

'It was very interesting. Turns out that Ellie Price knows Gerry Dunne; he helps at the church. She even has a photo of him in her house.'

'You think she might have hired him to kill Steve?' asked Kate.

'She certainly had motive, but I don't see it. There is one more thing, though, that's praying on my mind.'

'What's that?'

'Ellie told me that her priest, Father Anthony Moss, is a family friend of the Dunnes. He got them settled over here when they moved from Belfast. It seems he's taken Gerry under his wing.'

'The arrests will come as a big shock to him, then,' observed Kate.

Matt pursed his lips in thought. 'Somehow I doubt it, but let's see what he has to say for himself, shall we?'

# FORTY-EIGHT

Kate peered through the tall wrought-iron gates to get sight of the house; set back in the shadows of the ancient trees around it was a double-fronted Victorian building with large, cream painted sash windows. Ivy had spread across most of the front wall. The gate squeaked as Matt unlatched it, and she followed him through and closed it behind them. Her eyes darted left and right as her shoes crunched through the deep gravel. There was a silver Vauxhall Carlton on the drive; as she passed it, she alerted Matt to the leather holdall on the back seat. Matt nodded his acknowledgement and pushed the button on the front door, which chimed like church bells. They waited for a minute before trying again, but there was still no answer.

'Let's see if he's in the back,' said Matt, walking towards the wooden side gate and opening it.

'Are you sure? He might think we're trying to break in.'

'Come on, I'll lead the way.'

As they entered the overgrown back garden, Kate could hear birds singing in celebration of the sunshine. The warmth made her whole body feel nimble as she picked her way along a slabbed path between dense bushes, following a few paces behind Matt. Two crows flew off from a maple tree as they came through a clearing to a garden shed, its door left wide open. As she passed behind a giant rhododendron, she heard a faint click from behind. She recognised the sound at once. Her body stiffened as the point of a gun knifed into her back. A deep Irish voice barked out. 'Move one more inch and you're dead.'

She stopped in her tracks and saw Matt ahead, turning around, a look of horror on his face. 'That goes for you too,' said the voice at her back. Her body was trembling like a leaf in a hurricane. Matt was six feet away from her, his hands raised in the air.

'Let her go, Father,' said Matt, in a firm voice.

'I warned you what would happen if you didn't back off,' said the priest.

'Planning to make a run for it, are you?' asked Matt. 'It's too late for that I'm afraid; the police are on to you.'

'You're bluffing, Crawford. The police don't even know you're here, do they?'

'Of course they do,' replied Matt, 'they'll be here any minute.'

The priest sniggered. 'I don't believe you. Gerry would never—'

'That's where you're wrong. Gerry talked. They know everything,' said Matt with a defiant stare.

Sirens could be heard in the distance; they were getting louder. Kate felt the point of the gun being released from her spine. Matt still had a steely glare on his face.

'Gerry talked,' muttered the priest under his breath as he edged away from Kate, pistol in hand. She heard his shoes brushing through the long grass before he came into vision again. He stood to the side, an equal distance from her and Matt. He waved the gun in Matt's direction, then towards her. Matt, hands still raised, mouthed the words "keep still", but she couldn't stop the trembling in her hands, even when the priest lowered the pistol and held it at his side. When she did risk a glance in his direction, she saw that Father Anthony was no longer looking at her. He was staring straight out into nothingness, a wildness in his eyes. 'I will not let them arrest me. I must put myself in the hands of God and pray he will forgive me,' he said in a solemn voice. He stood bolt upright and, for a few seconds, there was only the sound of his deep breathing.

'Don't do it, Father,' bawled Kate, breaking the silence.

Her words didn't seem to register. The priest was completely absorbed in his own thoughts. When he spoke, his voice had changed to the deep monotone of an incantation. '*Fili, mox in caelis erimus.*' He made the sign of the cross, and as he raised the gun to his temple, Matt rushed towards him. It was too late; the priest had already pulled the trigger. In an explosion of brain tissue and blood, he collapsed onto the earth.

Kate felt a sudden dizziness; her vision blacked out. She couldn't stop herself falling, but she didn't hit the ground. When she came round, her eyes were blurred and sore from tears. It was like waking from the worst of bad dreams in the night. Her heart was racing, thumping in her chest. As her eyes began to clear, she saw she was sitting on a garden bench encircled by Matt's strong arms. 'Kate, it's going to be alright,' he said in a calming voice. 'I'm here – it's over.'

# DAY SEVENTEEN

Wednesday, 13 April 1983

# FORTY-NINE

Darkness had fallen and Matt and Kate were curled up on his sofa drinking wine, music playing in the background. It was a double celebration. The Mackie file was closed, and Luke had finally signed the divorce papers. Matt had his arm around her shoulder, and she tilted her head up to look into his eyes.

'How was Hazel when you saw her?' she asked.

'Still very shocked. She was convinced it was all about money. When I told her about Father Anthony, the colour drained from her face.'

'I can't believe it. She blames herself for Steve's murder?'

'Yes. She said that if she hadn't told Ellie Price the truth about the accident, none of this would have happened.'

'But that's ridiculous.'

'That's exactly what I said.'

'Poor Hazel,' said Kate, with sad eyes. 'It's going to be hard for her to get her head around everything that's happened. Come to think of it, there are a few things I'd like you to explain to *me* too. For a start, how *did* you work out that Father Anthony was Carl Price's dad?'

'His last words. They translate as "son, soon we will be reunited in heaven".'

'How did you know he meant Carl when he said it?' asked Kate.

'I remembered what Ellie had said to you. That Carl's father couldn't marry her and had made her promise not to tell a soul about his identity. It would have meant an end to his priesthood. He chose faith over fatherhood. And he could never forgive the person who had killed his own flesh and blood. He could not forgive the lies about the accident and the way Steve tried to pin the blame on Carl. And he could not forget that Steve had seduced his former lover, Ellie, and taken her money.'

'Did Ellie know what Father Anthony had done?' asked Kate.

'She says she had no idea and I believe her.'

'Another thing I'm curious about. Did you really call the police to Father Anthony's house, or were you bluffing?'

'No, I didn't. The sirens were a big stroke of luck.'

She drew away from him. 'Bloody hell, Matt. We could have been killed.'

'I would never have let that happen; I can assure…' The lounge door creaked open, making him hesitate, but for once, he felt no sense of panic. As it turned out, it was Desmond back from his nightly prowl.

'You were brave, I'll give you that,' said Kate. 'I'm curious about how the police got Tamara to talk?'

'Joe Martin offered her a reduced sentence.'

'How do you feel about that?' she asked, moving a little closer again.

He sipped more wine as he thought. 'I'm not sure. Maybe it was worth it to get the whole story.'

'What did Tamara tell them exactly?'

'She explained that Father Anthony offered her and her brother five grand to kill Steve Mackie. She said it wasn't all about the money; they owed the priest for getting them out of Northern Ireland. I'm not so sure. Anyway, they agreed, and Gerry and Tamara came up with a plan for the perfect murder. Father Anthony had told them about Steve's mounting debts and so they planned to make it look like suicide. Gerry knew Colin Mason from his days as a bouncer. He knew he was down on his luck and needed the money. Colin gladly agreed to play the part of house viewer. Gerry and Tamara were waiting outside in the van. Once Steve and Colin were inside, they pounced. Steve was tied and gagged.'

'Then what?' asked Kate.

'They waited for night to fall, then took Mackie down to the river. That's when Tamara crashed the van into the fence; there are no lights down there and she lost the towpath. They had drugged and bound Steve and were going to tie rocks to his legs to weigh him down. Colin and Gerry had dragged him to the riverbank, but Steve came round and managed to loosen the ropes around his wrists. Evidence suggests they used his tie to gag him. He must have thrown it off into the reeds after breaking free. Colin tried to stop him getting away and, during the fight, Steve hit him over the head with one of the rocks, pushed him into the river and ran off into the woods. Gerry chased after him and shot him in the back. He and Tamara covered Steve's body with loose earth and headed out, dumping the van near Trent Lock. They came back in Gerry's car at first light to bury the body and clear up the scene.'

'But they missed the tie. Enter Detective M.G. Crawford, stage left.'

'Exactly.'

'By the way, what *does* the G stand for?' she asked.

A flush crept across Matt's cheeks. 'I suppose we've known each other long enough now. It's Goodwill.'

She laughed. 'You're joking, that's not a name.'

'It is in Yorkshire; that's where my grandad comes from. I was named after him.'

'Do you have any more family secrets?'

'I don't think so. But there is something I've been wanting to ask *you* for some time.'

She stroked his arm. 'Really? What's that?'

'Apart from chocolate, what's your favourite food?'

She gave a heavy sigh; it was not the question she had hoped for. 'That's a tough one. Fish I suppose.'

'Great. Shall we go to the chip shop after?'

Kate looked up at him and frowned. 'On one condition.'
'What's that?'

'You change this record. What is it, anyway?'

'Desmond Dekker and The Aces. Thought you liked them.'

# ACKNOWLEDGEMENTS

Thanks: firstly to my wife Jill, for reading every chapter multiple times and giving me the encouragement to carry on; to Carol and Steve Pottinger for their valuable feedback on the manuscript; to Steve Dunne for his expert advice on the novel's opening chapters; and to Katherine Buttfield, Mo and Martin Parker-Eames, Carol Rutherford and Misia Smith from the Smoking Pen writing group in Nottingham for their unwavering support of my writing.

# ABOUT THE AUTHOR

After graduating in Philosophy, I joined a Canadian aluminium company as a Press Officer. This involved writing press releases for technical journals and local and national newspapers. It was not my first media job. Before that I had been the voice behind the microphone at Lord's cricket ground. I stayed in the metals industry for most of my career, before retiring early to focus on writing. I grew up in the East Midlands and now live in Nottingham.

See my website nicksands.co.uk for more.

For exclusive discounts on Matador titles,
sign up to our occasional newsletter at
troubador.co.uk/bookshop